FORGOTTEN WORDS

By

TIM GUDITUS

TABLE OF CONTENTS

Dedication

To the unsung heroes of intelligence agencies worldwide, who operate in the shadows, making sacrifices for the sake of national security. To my brothers in the NYPD, and all brother officers. To those who walk the tightrope between right and wrong, and to those who bear the scars of their actions—both visible and unseen. This book is a testament to their unwavering dedication, their complex moral landscapes, and the often-unseen consequences of their choices. It is also dedicated to the resilience of the human spirit, its capacity for both profound darkness and unexpected redemption.

This story is not theirs, yet it reflects the echoes of countless untold tales—whispering of betrayal, sacrifice, and the enduring weight of secrets. For those who live on the knife's edge, may this story serve as a reminder of the price of their commitment and the enduring impact of their actions on a world forever shaped by the shadows of their existence.

It is further dedicated to all those who have suffered at the hands of terrorism and organized crime. May this book serve as a small tribute to their courage and resilience, and as a reminder of the fight against the darkness that still grips our world.

Finally, this book is dedicated to the enduring power of storytelling—the capacity of fiction to illuminate the darkest corners of the human experience and inspire reflection upon the complexities of our world.

The precinct buzzed—a chaotic symphony of ringing phones and shouting officers. My partner, Detective Miller, a man whose enthusiasm for police work peaked at ensuring a consistently fresh pot of coffee, was glued to his desk. He seemed content updating files while I, the golden boy of the Robbery Squad, was left to my own devices.

The Captain, recognizing my efficiency, had granted me unprecedented autonomy. My cases—violent and thrilling—were clearing faster than I could log them. This freedom, however, came at a cost.

"Detective Miller," a gruff voice cut through the noise, "you got a call." The officer held out the phone, his eyes momentarily leaving his paperwork.

I took the phone. "Pickens," I answered.

"You're screwing my girl, Pickens," the voice snarled.

It was Sharon Cohen—the ex-rogue Mossad agent, the murderer I'd been chasing, and Miriam's ex-boyfriend.

"And I'm gonna make you pay."

The line went dead.

My affair with Miriam was reckless. I knew it. The NYPD's guidelines on fraternization were clear. But the physical intensity between us—the way our bodies intertwined, seeming to form a single entity—made caution an impossible burden. Miriam's dark skin, the warmth of her embrace, the way we made love—it overshadowed all rational thought.

I found myself regularly visiting her apartment alone at night. Every time, the risk felt more palpable.

"That was... interesting," Miller commented, his voice flat. "Should we report that?"

I shrugged. "He's just blowing off steam. Besides, I doubt he'd be able to prove anything."

The lie felt slick in my mouth.

Later, back on patrol, the city felt different—more menacing. Every shadow seemed to hold a threat. The adrenaline from the chase, the satisfaction of apprehending a suspect, was replaced by a constant, nagging fear. The work, usually a welcome escape, only amplified the unease.

"Another jewelry heist downtown," my radio crackled. "Two suspects, armed and dangerous."

This was it. The thrill of the chase, the intoxicating danger, the chance to momentarily forget Miriam and the weight of my actions. This was my drug, and I was hooked.

I drove to the scene, my heart pounding—not entirely from adrenaline, but also from the fear of Marco's threat. The scene was chaotic—sirens blaring, witnesses pointing—but I focused, my training taking over. My partner, Miller, was taking notes from the safety of the perimeter.

"Diaz, you okay?" Miller asked as I returned from apprehending one suspect.

"Yeah," I said, but the lie tasted bitter this time. I knew I needed to end the affair. The risk to my career—and worse, my safety—was too great. But the thought of losing Miriam... that was another burden.

The next day, I found Miriam's apartment empty. A note rested on the table. It was brief—just her name and a single phone number. A new number. She was gone. No goodbye. No explanation. Just a phone number.

I stared at the number, then at the phone in my hand. The precinct was quiet. Miller was absorbed in his coffee, the sounds of the city muted. The thrill of the chase was gone.

All that was left was the emptiness—the void left by a reckless affair and the uneasy silence of a life gone wrong.

"Miller," I said, my voice barely a whisper. "I need a transfer. Out of Robbery." He looked up, a hint of surprise on his face. He simply nodded and went back to his coffee. The transfer was surprisingly easy to arrange. It was as if the Captain had anticipated this request. It would be a clean break. Or so I hoped.

The precinct buzzed—a chaotic symphony of ringing phones and clattering typewriters. My partner, Detective Miller, a man whose dedication to paperwork far outweighed his enthusiasm for fieldwork, was hunched over his desk, the aroma of freshly brewed coffee battling the stale scent of old files. He barely registered my presence as I slipped out, leaving my half-empty mug beside his, a silent farewell. The freedom the Captain had granted me was a double-edged sword. My clearance rate was stellar, but the solo work felt isolating, especially with the weight of my affair with Miriam pressing down.

"Pickens," a gruff voice cut through my thoughts. It was Sergeant Davies, his face etched with a weariness that mirrored my own. "Got a new one. Jewelry store heist on Bleecker. Looks like a pro job."

"On it, Sarge," I replied, the adrenaline already pumping.

The robbery squad was my drug—the chase, the apprehension, the puzzle of the crime scene—it was intoxicating. But even the thrill of the hunt couldn't completely silence the echoes of Miriam's laughter, the feel of her skin against mine.

Later, back at my desk, my phone rang. A number I didn't recognize.

"Pickens," I answered, already bracing myself.

"You're messing with my girl, cop," a voice hissed, low and menacing. "This is Marco. And you're gonna regret it." The line went dead.

My heart hammered against my ribs. Marco. Miriam's ex. He'd made his threat clear.

The next few days blurred into a chaotic mix of stakeouts, interrogations, and the ever-present threat hanging over me. I managed to track down the Bleecker Street robbers—a surprisingly clean operation—but the success felt hollow. The constant fear gnawed at me—the fear of Marco, the fear of exposure, the fear of losing Miriam.

One evening, I met Miriam at our usual spot—a dimly lit Italian restaurant tucked away on a quiet side street.

"Tommy, you seem tense," Miriam observed, her hand reaching across the table to cover mine. "Is it the work?"

"It's more than the work, Miriam," I admitted, my voice barely a whisper. "Marco called me. He threatened me."

"Oh God," she whispered, her eyes wide with fear. "I should have told you…"

"Told me what?"

"He's… he's not as over me as he lets on," she confessed, her voice trembling. "He's still… possessive."

"Possessive is an understatement," I said. "He threatened my life on the phone, Miriam. This is serious."

"I'm sorry, Tommy. I'm so, so sorry," she sobbed, her dark eyes filled with tears. "I didn't want to put you in danger."

"Then let's end this," I said, the words heavy with a mixture of fear and exhaustion. The danger, the secrecy, the constant anxiety—it was all too much.

Silence hung between us, thick and suffocating. The aroma of the pasta dishes was lost in the heavy weight of our words. The affair had run its course, ending not with a bang, but with a quiet, fearful whisper in a dimly lit restaurant. The precinct life, with its inherent dangers, felt suddenly much more complicated, much lonelier. The thrill of the chase, once a drug, now felt like a bitter reminder of a reckless gamble I'd lost.

Preface

This novel delves into the treacherous world of espionage and international crime, exploring the moral ambiguities inherent in the pursuit of justice and the devastating consequences of betrayal. Detective Tommy Pickens, an intensive NYPD investigator, Sharon Cohen, our protagonist, is far from a traditional hero. He is a man driven by conflicting loyalties, shaped by the brutal realities of his profession, and haunted by the choices he's made. His journey is not one of simple redemption; instead, it's a descent into darkness, a harrowing exploration of the human capacity for both good and evil. Through Cohen's experiences, we examine the shadowy world of Mossad operations, the brutality of the Israeli mob, and the complex dynamics of Middle Eastern geopolitics. This is not a simple tale of good versus evil but a nuanced exploration of the gray areas where morality becomes blurred and the lines between right and wrong are deliberately obscured. The narrative aims to capture the visceral reality of life on the edge, the constant threat of violence, and the profound psychological toll of living a double life. The characters are flawed, their actions often driven by self-interest, yet their motivations are often rooted in a complex mix of ambition, loyalty, and the desperate pursuit of survival. This story unfolds against a backdrop of real-world events and locations, weaving together fact and fiction to create a compelling narrative that leaves the reader questioning the very nature of justice and the elusive concept of redemption. This is a story of shadows, betrayal, and the enduring power of the human spirit, even in the face of overwhelming adversity.

Introduction

Sharon Cohen, a former Mossad agent and once a rising star in the organization, finds himself adrift in a sea of betrayal and moral compromise. His disillusionment stems from a pivotal operation, "Operation Nightingale's Shadow," involving a thwarted Al-Qaeda bombing plot. The success of the operation, intertwined with the Israeli government's clandestine removal of gold reserves from the first World Trade Center bombing, leaves Cohen feeling deeply betrayed by the very organization he served. His undercover espionage, where he went deep undercover, helped with bombing advice, and traded as a bomb maker, schooled in explosives, further deepens his disillusionment. He kept in contact and warned his government of the possible bombing, causing an immediate stir. This betrayal fuels his descent into the criminal underworld, where he finds himself entangled with the Israeli mob in Morocco. He trades the cloak and dagger for the grim realities of drug trafficking and corruption. His path intersects with that of NYPD Detective Tommy Pickens, who investigates a series of murders and robberies, unwittingly drawing him into Cohen's dangerous web.

The plot thickens with the introduction of Miriam, Cohen's ex-girlfriend and a fellow spy, whose life becomes intertwined with both Cohen and Pickens, creating a volatile triangle of deceit, betrayal, and vengeance. As Cohen's violent acts escalate, targeting a diverse range of victims, including wealthy Israelis, Pakistani cab drivers, and even an element within the Muslim Brotherhood, the narrative intensifies, highlighting the intricate connections between international terrorism, organized crime, and the machinations of powerful governments.

The story unfolds through a first-person narrative, offering an intimate and unfiltered glimpse into Cohen's mind, allowing the reader to grapple with his morally ambiguous choices and the devastating consequences that follow. The story is a blend of high-stakes action, geopolitical intrigue, and character-driven drama, ultimately posing questions about loyalty, redemption, and the enduring power of the past to shape the present. The reader is invited to embark on a suspenseful journey through a world of secrets, lies, and the ever-present threat of violence, culminating in a climactic confrontation that will leave them questioning the very nature of justice and the elusive promise of redemption.

Operation Nightingales Shadow

Sharon Cohen, a Mossad agent, was in Casablanca. The air hung heavy, thick with the scent of salt and simmering resentment. It was July, and the city shimmered under a relentless sun, a perfect backdrop for the tensions that pulsed beneath the surface. My mission, codenamed Operation Nightingale, had begun six months earlier—a delicate dance on the razor's edge between loyalty and betrayal. The target: Al-Qaeda's nascent Moroccan cell, suspected of planning a devastating bombing targeting a high-profile Israeli delegation scheduled to visit Marrakech. My cover: a disillusioned Moroccan businessman, fluent in Arabic and Hebrew, with a penchant for expensive whiskey and even more expensive women.

The initial weeks were a blur of clandestine meetings, coded messages, and the constant, gnawing fear of discovery. I navigated the labyrinthine alleys of the medina, the crowded souks masking my movements like a chameleon blending into its surroundings. My handlers, back in Tel Aviv, were initially pleased with my progress. I had established a credible persona, gained the trust of several key operatives, and was privy to snippets of their increasingly frantic communications. Their plans were audacious, fueled by a potent cocktail of religious fervor and political desperation. The target, they boasted, would be a symbol of Israeli arrogance and a testament to their unwavering resolve.

But even then, a disquiet had begun to fester within me—a subtle erosion of the unwavering loyalty I had once felt towards Mossad. The orders were clear: gather intelligence, identify key players, and prevent the attack. But there was a chilling undercurrent, a sense of something more, something hidden beneath the surface of the official narrative. It began subtly: an uncharacteristic hesitation from my superiors, a cryptic message hinting at a larger operation beyond my immediate assignment.

The dissonance grew with each passing day. My contact, a wiry man named Omar, revealed more than he should have, his fervor for the cause masking a crippling lack of operational competence. Their bombs, I discovered, were crude, prone to malfunction, and far less sophisticated than I had been led to believe. They were desperate, reckless, and frankly, their execution was amateurish. It made me wonder: was this truly a matter of imminent threat, or was something else at play?

The doubts intensified when I discovered the true scope of Operation Nightingale. It wasn't just about preventing a terrorist attack. It was about something far more insidious—something that would shake the foundations of my world. My superiors, it seemed, were not just concerned with thwarting a bombing. They were orchestrating a play on a much larger scale, using the threat of terrorism as a smokescreen for a covert operation of their own. I stumbled upon it accidentally, a casual conversation overheard in a dimly lit Marrakech café—a hushed discussion that chilled me to the bone.

The conversation was about the gold. Tons of it, housed in the World Trade Center. Israeli gold, a strategic reserve, a national treasure. And it was being moved secretly, under the guise of the impending terrorist attack. The bombing, a carefully constructed pretext for a preemptive strike, a financial maneuver cloaked in the urgency of national security. The implication was devastating. The very organization I had dedicated my life to, the one I had sworn to serve, was manipulating a global crisis for its own economic gain.

This revelation shattered my carefully constructed world. The moral ambiguity that had always been a part of espionage had morphed into something far more sinister, something irredeemable. The line between justice and injustice blurred, dissolving into a murky swamp of deceit and self-preservation. The sacrifice of potentially innocent lives, all to protect a national asset, felt like a betrayal not only of my own values but also of the ideals I had once held dear.

The seed of disillusionment had been planted, and it grew quickly, twisting its roots deep into my soul. Operation Nightingale, far from being a heroic mission, was a calculated act of manipulation—a reckless game played with lives as pawns. I had been a tool, unwittingly complicit in a clandestine operation that used fear and violence to mask a far more nefarious agenda. The knowledge gnawed at me, a relentless tide of betrayal that threatened to consume me entirely.

The official narrative of thwarted terrorism, the accolades bestowed upon Mossad, the pat on the back from my superiors—it all felt sickeningly hollow, a grotesque parody of justice. My role in it was a stain I couldn't wash away. The decision to leave Mossad wasn't a choice; it was a desperate act of self-preservation, a desperate attempt to escape the suffocating weight of complicity.

Leaving wasn't easy. Mossad doesn't let go of its assets easily. The threats were subtle at first—a menacing phone call, a shadowed figure lingering near my apartment. Then the violence began: a car accident, meticulously staged to look like an accident. An anonymous package filled with a noxious substance, designed not to kill but to terrorize. The game had shifted from covert operations to a brutal power struggle, a war waged in the shadows. It was a fight for my life, a fight for my soul. And I was losing.

The allure of the Moroccan underworld, with its promises of anonymity and freedom from the constraints of my past, became an irresistible siren song. I traded my tailored suits for worn leather jackets, my sophisticated weaponry for a more brutal arsenal. I had gone from a trained operative to a ruthless mercenary, selling my skills to the highest bidder.

My former life as a Mossad agent provided me with an advantage, but it also marked me, turning me into a target. The shadows of the past stretched out like grasping claws, threatening to pull me under. My life, once dedicated to the pursuit of justice, had become a twisted reflection of the very thing I had sworn to oppose. The descent was swift and brutal, a spiraling vortex of violence and self-destruction.

The Israeli mob in Morocco, a network of ruthless criminals operating with impunity, became my new employers. They provided the resources, the connections, the anonymity I craved. The life was brutal, morally bankrupt, and deeply intoxicating. I trafficked drugs, laundered money, and indulged in acts of violence I hadn't even imagined committing. Each act was a deeper plunge into the abyss, a chipping away at whatever remained of my former morality. I became numb to the violence, the death, the corruption. It was a brutal existence, a twisted reflection of my earlier life, but without the veneer of patriotism or ideological justification.

The final act of betrayal, the one that would cement my fall from grace, was the assault on Miriam. She had been my lover, my confidante, my equal in the shadowy world of espionage. But my descent into darkness had left no room for loyalty, no space for sentiment. My actions were fueled by a mixture of rage, betrayal, and cold, calculating self-preservation. I had used her, discarded her, and then, when she threatened to expose my new life, I silenced her. Leaving her broken and bleeding, both physically and emotionally, marked the point of no return. The moral compass that had once guided me, however faintly, was shattered beyond repair. The man I once was was gone, replaced by a cold, calculating monster. And that monster was about to make a terrible mistake.

The Vanishing Gold Reserves

The sting of betrayal was a slow burn, a relentless erosion of trust that gnawed at me long after the brutal assault on Miriam. It wasn't just the physical act—the sickening crunch of bone, the crimson blossoming across her pale skin—it was the chilling realization that the government I'd served, the nation I'd sworn to protect, had betrayed me far more deeply than I'd betrayed her. The seeds of that realization had been sown months earlier, during Operation Nightingale, but it wasn't until later, shrouded in the Moroccan haze of my new criminal life, that the full picture sharpened into focus.

It began subtly, a whisper in the back of my mind, a nagging inconsistency. The frantic, almost desperate nature of the orders surrounding the Israeli delegation's visit to Marrakech. The sheer volume of intelligence resources dedicated to thwarting a relatively small Al-Qaeda cell—it didn't quite fit the profile. Then came the gold. Not the glittering, ostentatious gold of the jewelry trade, but the cold, hard, unyielding gold of national reserves. Tons of it. Shifted, under the guise of routine financial transactions, from the bowels of the World Trade Center, just days before the meticulously planned Al-Qaeda attack that I'd helped prevent.

The official explanation was ludicrous—a routine audit, a necessary relocation to secure assets. But my gut, honed by years in the field, screamed otherwise. I had seen the fear in the eyes of the high-ranking officials involved. I'd felt the tremor of deception in their carefully constructed words. The same deceptive undercurrents that rippled through the dark waters of Casablanca. It wasn't just a coincidence. It was a carefully orchestrated charade, a preemptive strike designed to cover up something far more sinister. The attack became a conveniently timed distraction, a smokescreen for the disappearance of a national treasure.

My access, granted through the intricacies of Operation Nightingale, gave me a glimpse behind the curtain. I had access to encrypted communications, secure servers, and financial records that would have made a lesser man tremble. Slowly, painstakingly, I pieced together the truth. The Israeli government, in a move of breathtaking cynicism, had anticipated the Al-Qaeda attack and used the chaos as a cover to move a significant portion of its gold reserves, transferring the gold to a series of offshore accounts and shell corporations, far from the eyes of any potential investigators.

The audacity of it staggered me. To use a potential terrorist attack, a massacre of innocent lives, as cover for such blatant financial malfeasance was a perversion of state power on an unimaginable scale. The meticulous planning, the intricate web of deceit—it was the kind of operation only a government could pull off with such finesse, the kind of betrayal that could shake the foundations of a nation.

And I had been a pawn in this grand game. My loyalty, my sacrifice, my near-death experiences in the heart of a terrorist cell had all been used to facilitate the government's underhanded scheme. The knowledge twisted in my stomach, a bitter cocktail of outrage and self-loathing. They had used me, then discarded me like a soiled handkerchief.

No accolades, no recognition, no reward—only the bitter taste of betrayal.

The realization fueled the darkness that had already begun to consume me. The disillusionment that began with Miriam's assault deepened into a chasm of nihilism. If the government I had served could act with such breathtaking hypocrisy and disregard for human life, what was the point of loyalty? What was the point of anything?

My subsequent actions became a spiral of self-destruction, a reckless plunge into the murky depths of the criminal underworld. The drug deals, the protection rackets, the contract killings—they were not merely acts of greed or ambition. They were acts of defiance, a desperate attempt to reclaim some semblance of control in a world that had shattered my ideals and left me feeling utterly betrayed.

The Moroccan underworld provided the perfect refuge, a shadowy ecosystem where loyalty and betrayal were currency, and the lines between right and wrong blurred into oblivion. I operated in the shadows, a phantom in the labyrinthine streets of Casablanca, my former skills now used for profit rather than patriotism. The money, the power, the anonymity—it all served as a temporary balm for the festering wound of my betrayal. But the emptiness gnawed relentlessly. The ghost of Miriam haunted me, a constant reminder of the human cost of my descent. The ghost of my former self, the idealistic Mossad agent, whispered warnings from the margins of my consciousness.

The gold, however, remained a constant, insidious presence. It became a symbol of everything I despised, a physical manifestation of the rot at the heart of the system I had once served. Its very existence was a reminder of my complicity, my unwitting role in this colossal act of state-sponsored larceny. The knowledge of the stolen gold pulsed like a malignant tumor within me, a source of constant, gnawing pain. It fueled my cynicism, sharpened my ruthlessness, and solidified my decision to walk a path away from any form of redemption.

The wealth I accumulated through my criminal enterprises was a twisted mockery of the rewards I had been denied. It was stained with the blood of my victims, the tears of Miriam, and the silent screams of those whose lives had been sacrificed on the altar of Israeli state security. Yet, even this wealth couldn't fill the void within, a void that grew wider and deeper with each passing day.

The arrest, when it came, was almost an anticlimax. The years of living on the edge, the constant fear of exposure, the relentless pressure of my double life—they had worn me down. The wiretap on Miriam's phone, a cruel twist of irony, was the final piece of the puzzle. It led the NYPD, quite unexpectedly, to my doorstep. And to them, the ruthless, dangerous Cohen was, in essence, just another criminal.

They had no idea of the larger tapestry of deceit, the geopolitical chess game in which I had played such a devastatingly small role. They only saw a man who deserved to be locked away, a violent, brutal criminal. But in the cold, hard reality of my cell, my deepest regret wasn't the crimes I'd committed, but the betrayal I'd suffered—a betrayal far deeper and more insidious than any I'd ever inflicted. The gold, that cursed, glittering gold, lay somewhere in a distant, anonymous bank account, a monument to the deceit that had irrevocably destroyed my life and left me adrift in a sea of bitterness and regret. The price of betrayal, it seemed, was a life spent paying.

Broken Oaths and Severed Ties

The Moroccan sun beat down on the dusty streets of Casablanca, a stark contrast to the sterile, climate-controlled offices of Mossad headquarters. The shift was jarring, brutal even, a physical manifestation of the chasm that had opened between my past and my present. I'd traded tailored suits and encrypted briefings for threadbare shirts and hushed whispers in dimly lit bars. The comforting weight of a Glock 17 had been replaced by the ever-present, gnawing anxiety of living outside the law.

My reasons for leaving Mossad were complex, a tangled web of disillusionment, betrayal, and a simmering sense of injustice. Operation Nightingale, the operation that had involved the clandestine removal of Israeli gold reserves from the World Trade Center before the Al-Qaeda bombing, was the catalyst. The meticulous planning, the dangerous infiltration, the near-misses—all culminated in a victory that was never acknowledged, a success that was subtly erased from the official record. My contribution, my near-sacrifice, was deemed expendable, a footnote in a much larger narrative of political expediency.

The government's swift and silent appropriation of the gold reserves, a move that solidified their financial security while leaving me empty-handed and exposed, left a bitter taste in my mouth. This wasn't just a professional disappointment; it was a personal betrayal of epic proportions. The oaths I'd sworn, the loyalty I'd given, had been casually discarded like a used cigarette butt. It felt like a violation, not just of my professional integrity, but of my very soul.

The subsequent descent into the criminal underworld was almost inevitable. It wasn't a conscious decision, not initially, but a slow, insidious slide down a slippery slope. First, there were the small favors, the discreet transactions, the overlooked opportunities. Then came the bolder moves, the riskier ventures—drug trafficking, extortion, protection rackets. The Israeli mob in Morocco was a welcoming, albeit dangerous, fraternity. They understood the language of betrayal; they recognized the quiet desperation in my eyes. They saw the potential for profit, but more importantly, they saw the potential for destruction.

The Moroccan underworld was a brutal tapestry woven with threads of greed, corruption, and violence. I thrived in this chaotic environment, adopting a persona far removed from the disciplined, controlled operative I once was. This new identity, this carefully constructed mask, allowed me to exist, to function, to survive.

Miriam, my former lover and a fellow Mossad agent, was both a casualty and a catalyst in this metamorphosis. Our relationship, passionate and intense, had been built on shared secrets, mutual trust, and a profound understanding of the dangers inherent in our profession. But the chasm that separated us, the conflicting loyalties that divided us, eventually proved too wide to bridge. She was, unknowingly, a pawn in the political game, and in my descent into darkness, she became a victim.

The assault on Miriam wasn't a moment of impulsive rage, but a calculated act of self-preservation. She knew too much, and her proximity to the operation's aftermath made her a liability. Silencing her was a brutal but necessary measure, a grim testament to the amoral world I now inhabited. The physical act itself was horrific, a brutal violation that left me reeling with a mixture of guilt and chilling detachment. But it was a calculated action, a decision born from a place of deep, abiding fear and desperation. The thought of exposure, of my past catching up with me, was a constant, agonizing pressure.

The years that followed were a blur of illicit activities, fleeting relationships, and constant paranoia. The money flowed freely, but it brought no solace, no peace of mind. The luxurious villas, the fast cars, the endless supply of exotic drugs – they were all superficial comforts, hollow masks designed to conceal the emptiness that gnawed at my core. I lived on the edge of a razor blade, my senses hyper-alert to any sign of betrayal, any hint of impending danger.

My targets were diverse. Wealthy Israelis, oblivious to the true nature of their persecutor, became easy prey. Pakistani cab drivers, caught in the crossfire of my escalating criminal activities, became collateral damage. The escalating brutality of my actions reflected the deepening abyss within me, a chasm born from a profound sense of disillusionment and betrayal.

The contract to eliminate a member of the Muslim Brotherhood attempting to infiltrate the US government was the culmination of my descent. It was a final, desperate attempt to maintain my relevance, to prove my worth in a world that had rejected me. It was a mission shrouded in secrecy, a complex operation involving layers of deception and intricate planning. But even this, this final act, felt hollow, a desperate grasping at shadows.

The arrest was an anticlimactic end to a life lived on the edge. The wiretap on Miriam's phone, an ironic twist of fate, exposed my carefully constructed façade, unraveling years of deception and subterfuge. The NYPD, oblivious to the intricacies of the political machinations and global conspiracies that formed the backdrop of my life, simply saw a violent criminal—a dangerous man who needed to be locked away.

The gold, the cursed, glittering gold, remained a distant, unobtainable prize. It lay somewhere in an anonymous bank account, a tangible symbol of the deceit that had shattered my life, that had destroyed my trust in everything and everyone I'd once held dear. It was a chilling reminder of the oaths I'd broken, the ties I'd severed, and the price I would ultimately pay for my transgressions. The price of betrayal, as it turned out, was a life spent paying. The cold, steel bars of my cell were a fitting epitaph, a stark testament to a life consumed by disillusionment, betrayal, and a darkness that had become my only companion. The quiet hum of the prison ventilation system was a bleak counterpoint to the roar of my own self-loathing.

The Moroccan Underworld

The air hung thick and heavy, a miasma of sweat, dust, and the cloying sweetness of cheap perfume. Casablanca's medina, a labyrinth of twisting alleys and souks, was a far cry from the manicured lawns and sterile buildings of my former life. Here, survival wasn't about strategic planning and covert operations; it was about instinct, guile, and a ruthless willingness to exploit the weaknesses of others. My new employers, a loose confederation of Israeli mobsters operating under the guise of legitimate businesses, thrived in this chaos. They were sharks in a murky sea, their power built on fear, bribery, and an intricate network of informants spread throughout the city's underbelly.

My role was initially modest – managing the distribution of pharmaceuticals, mostly to satisfy the insatiable appetites of the city's wealthy elite and the less discerning masses. But soon, my skills proved invaluable. My experience in intelligence, my ability to read people, assess risk, and anticipate the moves of my opponents, made me indispensable. I quickly rose through the ranks, my ruthlessness silencing dissent and establishing my dominance within the group. The meticulously planned operations of Mossad were replaced by a more visceral, chaotic reality. Success here meant brutal efficiency, calculated risks, and an unwavering commitment to self-preservation.

One of my early tasks involved securing a shipment of heroin from a notoriously volatile supplier in Tangier. The man, a hulking brute named Omar, was known for his brutal methods and penchant for violence. The meeting took place in a dimly lit, smoke-filled café, the air thick with the tension of a potential showdown. Omar, surrounded by his heavily armed goons, was all bravado and menacing smiles. He'd underestimated me, however, mistaking my calm demeanor for weakness. I'd anticipated his every move, knowing the subtle nuances of his body language, the telltale signs of aggression masked behind a veneer of casual indifference. I played along, feigning compliance while subtly assessing the layout of the café, the angles of approach, and the escape routes.

The negotiation was tense, a silent war of wills played out across a scarred wooden table. In the end, it wasn't force that won the day, but a calculated display of confidence and a subtle hint of my own violent capabilities. A threat, veiled in a casual remark about shared acquaintances with "certain individuals" – individuals Omar understood to be well-versed in dispensing swift and brutal justice. The heroin was delivered, the deal successfully concluded, and my position strengthened.

The Moroccan underworld was a tapestry woven with threads of corruption, where the lines between legality and illegality blurred beyond recognition. Police officers, government officials, even certain elements within the judiciary were all compromised, their loyalty bought and sold with casual disregard for morality. This network of complicity facilitated the operation, offering a veil of protection that was as important as the armed guards. Bribes, carefully placed, greased the wheels of this corrupt machine.

My understanding of the intricate power dynamics of the region, acquired during my time with Mossad, was now proving to be an invaluable asset. I knew who to pay, when to pay them, and how to make sure the money remained untraceable.

Beyond the drugs, my activities diversified into other realms of organized crime – extortion, protection rackets, and even contract killings. Each mission was a carefully orchestrated dance of deception, where the slightest misstep could have fatal consequences. The adrenaline was a constant companion, a drug as potent as anything I trafficked. The thrill of the chase, the calculated risk, the sense of power that came with successfully pulling off an intricate scheme – it was addictive, a vortex that consumed me, leaving me craving more.

I targeted wealthy Israelis, exploiting their vulnerabilities, their greed, and their arrogance. They were easy prey, their lives insulated from the harsh realities of the world outside their gilded cages. Oblivious to the dangers they attracted, they were blind to the shadows lurking in their opulent villas and luxury hotels. I exploited this naivety, stripping them bare, leaving them financially and emotionally ruined. My methods were ruthless, often violent, and always effective. There was a certain perverse satisfaction in dismantling the carefully constructed lives of those who believed themselves untouchable.

But my activities extended beyond the Israeli community. Pakistani cab drivers, working long hours for meager wages, became another target. Their seemingly mundane lives concealed a vulnerability I was quick to exploit. I manipulated them with fabricated stories, promises of riches, and the ever-present threat of violence. These acts, though less glamorous than my operations against the wealthy Israelis, served a purpose – they maintained my position, strengthened my reputation, and kept the cash flow steady.

The moral compass that had once guided my actions, albeit within the often murky world of espionage, had long since atrophied. The cold, hard reality of survival on the streets had eroded any lingering sense of decency. The betrayal of Miriam, my former girlfriend, had been the ultimate breaking point. The brutal assault, the subsequent act of betrayal, had erased any vestige of the man I once was. The guilt gnawed at me, a persistent, nagging ache that I numbed with more work, more violence, and more money.

But even my self-destructive spiral had its limits. The sheer exhaustion, the constant vigilance, the never-ending cycle of betrayal and violence – it began to take its toll. The masks I wore, the personas I adopted to protect myself, grew heavy, stifling. I felt myself becoming increasingly isolated, disconnected from any semblance of normalcy. The only connection I craved – the only connection I allowed myself – was to the next deal, the next hit, the next surge of adrenaline that momentarily masked the profound emptiness inside. The relentless pursuit of money had left me hollowed out, a shell of the man I once was. The ghost of the man I wanted to be haunted me relentlessly.

My next assignment was to eliminate a member of the Muslim Brotherhood, someone who had infiltrated the upper echelons of the U.S. government. The details were scant, the information delivered through a series of coded messages and encrypted communications. This assignment differed from my previous undertakings – this was not about profit but about serving a larger, more sinister purpose. The shadowy figures pulling the strings remained unknown, their motives inscrutable. It was a dangerous game, one where the stakes were impossibly high, and the consequences could be catastrophic. But the challenge, the thrill of facing an unknown enemy, the potential for impact – these were the only things that still held my interest. The work was a means to escape my own self-hatred, a temporary reprieve from the ceaseless gnawing of guilt and regret. Little did I know, this contract would be the catalyst for my downfall. The threads of my past, carefully interwoven, were about to unravel, pulling me down into a darkness far deeper than anything I had ever experienced.

Betrayal and Violence

The cheap Moroccan whiskey burned a path down my throat, a fiery trail mirroring the turmoil inside me. Miriam's face, contorted in a mask of pain and fear, flickered behind my eyelids. The memory, sharp and brutal, clawed at my conscience, a phantom limb of guilt. It hadn't been a planned assault; it had been a descent, a slow, agonizing slide into the abyss of my own making. It started with an argument, a bitter exchange fueled by alcohol and the simmering resentment that had been poisoning our relationship for months. She'd discovered some of my activities, a few scraps of information gleaned from intercepted communications, enough to paint a disturbing picture of the man I'd become. Her accusations, though partially true, felt like a betrayal. A betrayal not just of our relationship, but of the ideals we once shared. The ideals I had long since abandoned.

The argument escalated, fueled by my own self-loathing. The years of clandestine operations, the moral compromises, the slow erosion of my humanity – it all came crashing down in that cramped apartment, a suffocating pressure cooker of anger and despair. I remember the feel of her skin beneath my hands, the desperate struggle, the sickening crunch of bone. The silence that followed was deafening, punctuated only by the erratic thump-thump-thump of my own heart, a frantic drumbeat against the backdrop of my own self-condemnation. The violence wasn't premeditated; it was an explosion, a release of pent-up rage and frustration directed at the one person who still saw the ghost of the man I used to be.

I left her there, a crumpled heap on the worn rug, her breath coming in ragged gasps. The image seared itself into my memory, a brand of shame that burned hotter than any desert sun. I didn't look back. I simply walked away, leaving behind the wreckage of our relationship, the shattered remnants of a love betrayed. The guilt was a constant companion, a venomous serpent coiled around my heart, its fangs sinking deeper with each passing day. It was a weight I carried, a burden I couldn't escape. It was a reminder of the darkness that had consumed me, a testament to the moral bankruptcy I had embraced.

The following days were a blur of frantic activity, a desperate attempt to outrun the ghosts that haunted me. I immersed myself in my work, burying myself in the gritty realities of the Casablanca underworld. The adrenaline rush of each new deal, each successful con, offered a temporary reprieve from the gnawing pain of my conscience. But it was a hollow victory, a fleeting illusion of control in a life increasingly spiraling out of control. The money flowed freely, but it couldn't buy redemption. It couldn't erase the image of Miriam's terror, the sound of her broken whimper.

My contact, a hulking man named Avraham with eyes like chips of obsidian, didn't ask about the incident. He didn't need to. The ruthlessness inherent in my actions spoke for itself. He merely issued my next assignment: a wealthy Israeli businessman, a diamond smuggler operating out of a seemingly legitimate jewelry store in the heart of the city.

The details were simple: eliminate the target, collect the payment. There was no moral quandary, no agonizing deliberation. It was just business. Or so I tried to convince myself.

The operation was executed with cold efficiency. I moved like a phantom, a shadow slipping through the city's labyrinthine streets. The target was found alone in his opulent apartment, surrounded by the glittering spoils of his illicit trade. His death was swift, almost painless, a quick, clean execution that left no trace. I collected the payment—a small fortune in untraceable diamonds—and vanished into the anonymity of the city's teeming masses. I felt nothing—not regret, not satisfaction. Just emptiness. The numbness was a shield, a protection against the ever-present ache of guilt that threatened to overwhelm me.

The subsequent weeks were a haze of drugs, alcohol, and casual violence. My life had become a self-destructive spiral, a reckless abandonment of any semblance of morality. I targeted Pakistani cab drivers, petty criminals, anyone who crossed my path and offered an opportunity for violence. It was a means of self-punishment, a twisted form of atonement for the wrongs I had committed. Each act of violence was a self-inflicted wound, a desperate attempt to numb the pain. The pain was not just the physical pain of the injuries I inflicted on the victims, but the emotional and psychological pain caused by the actions I had taken against Miriam.

But even the relentless pursuit of oblivion couldn't silence the whispers of my conscience. The shadow of Miriam's face continued to haunt me, a constant reminder of the man I had become. The emptiness deepened, a vast, echoing void that no amount of money, drugs, or violence could fill. The thrill of the chase, the adrenaline rush of danger, had become a dull ache, a hollow echo of its former intensity. I was adrift in a sea of despair, a ship without sails, caught in a storm of my own making.

The contract to eliminate the element within the Muslim Brotherhood was different. This wasn't about money or the fleeting satisfaction of violence. This was about something larger, something sinister. The details were vague, the instructions cryptic. All I knew was that the target was high-level, operating within the American government, and his exposure would have catastrophic consequences. The shadows were longer, the stakes higher. This assignment wasn't about personal gain, but about serving a force far greater than myself, a force I had yet to fully comprehend. The nature of this force, its aims and motivations, remained shrouded in mystery; yet, it held a chilling power. It was an allure that pulled me further into the darkness. I had been here before. Earlier, I had infiltrated Al-Qaeda during the first World Trade Center bombing—this would be a piece of cake.

Mossad is a highly secretive, powerful intelligence agency within the Israeli government. The organization is responsible for gathering and analyzing intelligence to protect Israel's national security interests. Over the years, Mossad has developed a reputation for being one of the most effective and ruthless intelligence agencies in the world, often using covert operations and assassinations to achieve its goals. The agency is also known for its ability to recruit and run highly skilled agents, many of whom have served in the Israeli military. Al-Qaeda, on the other hand, is a global militant Islamist organization founded by Osama bin Laden in the late 1980s. The group is known for its extremist ideologies and its involvement in terrorist attacks, including the September 11th attacks on the United States. Al-Qaeda's main goal is to establish a pan-Islamic caliphate through violent means, and the group has carried out numerous attacks on Western targets to achieve this goal. Despite the death of its leader, Al-Qaeda remains a threat to global security and continues to inspire and support terrorist activities around the world. The

Muslim Brotherhood, founded in 1928, is a transnational Islamist organization that advocates for the establishment of Islamic states based on sharia law. The group has a strong presence in the Middle East and North Africa and has been involved in political and social movements in many countries. The Muslim Brotherhood promotes a conservative and traditional interpretation of Islam and has been accused of using violence to achieve its goals. The organization has faced significant pushback from governments and other groups but continues to be a powerful force in the region. The NYPD, or New York City Police Department, is the largest municipal police force in the United States. With over 36,000 officers, the NYPD is responsible for law enforcement and public safety in the five boroughs of New York City. The department has a long history of protecting and serving the city and has faced numerous challenges and controversies over the years. Despite these challenges, the NYPD remains a vital institution in New York City and plays a crucial role in maintaining the safety and security of its citizens.

This new assignment was a dangerous game, a high-stakes gamble with my life. I prepared meticulously, gathering intelligence, studying the target's movements, plotting every detail of the operation. But even the meticulous planning couldn't mask the gnawing fear that something was wrong, that I was playing a game with rules I didn't fully understand. This was the final act of my story, and I was starting to suspect that the play was already written, the ending decided long before the first act ever began. My sense of foreboding intensified as I considered the consequences of this operation. I was walking into a dark, unknowable territory, where the lines between right and wrong were blurred, and the shadows held secrets far more deadly than any I had yet encountered.

The assignment itself became a blur of tense surveillance, whispered conversations, and close calls. I lived in the shadows, a ghost haunting the corridors of power, my movements unseen, my presence unheard. The target was elusive, a phantom flitting through the upper echelons of American society. The closer I got, the more I realized the depth of the conspiracy, the vastness of the web I was caught in. It wasn't just about eliminating one man; it was about unraveling a network of deceit and treachery that stretched across continents and touched the highest levels of government. The deeper I delved, the more dangerous the game became. I was playing with fire, and I knew, with chilling certainty, that I would soon be burned.

The final confrontation was brutal, a chaotic ballet of violence and betrayal. The target, a seemingly innocuous bureaucrat, proved to be far more dangerous than I had anticipated. The ensuing struggle was fierce, a desperate fight for survival in a darkened alley. The fight was not one of wits or skill; rather, it was a fight for survival, a fight against an enemy armed with political power and seemingly unlimited resources. The battle ended not with a clean kill, but with a near miss, a desperate escape in the shadow of imminent doom. This near miss, however, was to be my salvation. It was during this escape that I was inadvertently caught on a wiretap—the final piece of the puzzle that would lead to my downfall. The wiretap wasn't meant to capture my voice; it was part of a larger surveillance operation targeting my ex-girlfriend, Miriam. The irony was not lost on me. The woman I had betrayed, the woman I had violently assaulted, inadvertently became the instrument of my capture. The threads of my past, long tangled and interwoven, were finally beginning to unravel. My meticulously planned escape turned into a trap; the walls of my world were collapsing around me. My time in the shadows was drawing to an abrupt end.

Converging Paths

The flickering neon sign of a bodega cast a sickly yellow glow on Detective Tommy Pickens's rain-slicked trench coat. The chill November air bit at his exposed skin, a sharp contrast to the stifling heat of the cramped apartment he'd just left. The victim, a Pakistani cab driver named Anwar Khan, lay sprawled amidst a shattered coffee table and overturned chairs, a single, precise gunshot wound to the head. It was the third such murder in as many weeks, each victim sharing a similar profile: middle-aged, male, and of Middle Eastern or South Asian descent. The only other common thread was the complete absence of forced entry.

Pickens ran a hand through his already disheveled dark hair, the frustration palpable. This wasn't some gangland turf war; this was surgical, almost clinical. His partner, a fresh-faced rookie named Diaz, hovered nervously in the doorway, his notepad clutched like a lifeline. "Anything, Detective?"

Pickens sighed, pushing away the stray strands of hair clinging to his forehead. "Nothing but more questions, Diaz. No witnesses, no forced entry, pristine execution. It's like he walks in, does his business, and vanishes into thin air." He knelt beside the body, meticulously examining the scene.

The apartment was small, sparsely furnished, but meticulously clean. No signs of struggle, no forced entry, no discernible motive beyond the obvious: death. The only unusual item was a small, intricately carved wooden box tucked away in a dusty corner of the closet.

"The M.O. is consistent with the other two," Diaz offered, his voice barely a whisper. "Same type of weapon, same precision, same lack of evidence."

Pickens nodded, his gaze fixed on the box. It was ornate, almost beautiful, crafted from dark, polished wood inlaid with mother-of-pearl. He picked it up carefully, turning it over in his hands. It was locked, but the lock looked surprisingly flimsy. He figured a simple lock pick would open it easily. He pocketed the box, knowing it might hold a clue, however insignificant it might seem at the moment.

Back at the precinct, the box yielded little. Inside, nestled on a bed of faded velvet, was a single, tarnished silver coin, bearing an unfamiliar inscription. The only thing it held that resonated with Pickens was a renewed sense of unease. The methodical precision of the killings, the choice of victims, the almost artistic nature of the crime scene... it all pointed to someone with a high level of skill and a chilling sense of purpose. Someone who was meticulous, calculated, and utterly ruthless.

The next few days were a blur of interviews, stakeouts, and dead ends. Pickens immersed himself in the investigation, fueled by black coffee and a growing sense of dread. The victims, though seemingly disparate, were all connected in some way. Pickens was sure of it. He spent hours poring over their backgrounds, their financial records, their personal lives. He found nothing to link them until he discovered a surprising connection: each victim had been involved in some form of transaction with Israeli businessmen, albeit indirectly. This wasn't just random killings. This was targeted.

Meanwhile, his personal life was becoming increasingly complicated. He'd met Miriam, Sharon Cohen's ex-girlfriend, at a support group for victims of violent crime. Miriam was still recovering from the brutal attack—physically and emotionally scarred, haunted by the events. She was beautiful, intelligent, and fiercely independent, and despite the inherent risks, Pickens found himself drawn to her. The more he learned about her, the more the puzzle pieces started to fit together. The attack on Miriam was far more than just a random act of violence; it was the key to unlocking the mystery surrounding the murders.

The connection between the murders and Miriam was subtle at first, a whisper in the shadows. But as Pickens delved deeper into the case, the evidence became undeniable. The targets, the precision of the killings, the almost theatrical nature of the crime scenes—they all echoed the cold, calculated style of someone intimately familiar with the world of espionage and violence. Someone like Sharon Cohen, Miriam's ex-boyfriend.

The more he investigated the financial records of the victims and Miriam's background, the more he learned about Sharon's illicit dealings. The Israeli mob, drug trafficking, corruption—it all painted a disturbing picture of a man operating on the fringes of society, a man who knew how to move without a trace. A man capable of both brutality and calculating precision. Pickens found a pattern. The victims were all connected to Cohen, either directly or indirectly.

Pickens's suspicions slowly crystallized into a chilling certainty. A faint but undeniable connection emerged between the meticulously cleaned crime scenes and Cohen's infamous modus operandi. The bodies, positioned with surgical precision, the eerie absence of witnesses, the lack of forced entry—all mirrored the strategies of a trained professional, a seasoned killer. The connection between the murders and

Cohen was no longer a mere suspicion; it was glaringly obvious, almost taunting in its clarity. It felt as if Cohen was deliberately leaving a trail, a breadcrumb path leading directly back to his violent past.

Though circumstantial, the evidence was steadily mounting. Pickens carefully documented each connection, each subtle link, meticulously constructing his case. He knew the danger he was in, treading carefully in a high-stakes game of cat and mouse with a cunning and ruthless adversary. Cohen was no ordinary criminal; he was a man of intellect and cold-blooded efficiency, one who had erased every trace of his crimes. But Pickens was no stranger to danger. Known for his relentless perseverance and sharp instincts, he had a reputation for uncovering the truth even when buried beneath layers of lies and deception. Yet, as the case unfolded, a new weight settled on his shoulders. He wasn't just solving a string of murders anymore; he was stepping into the shadowy world of international intrigue and organized crime—a world that had ensnared Miriam, and could just as easily entrap him.

The tarnished silver coin, tucked inside the wooden box, continued to haunt him—a cryptic message left behind by the killer. Pickens turned his attention to the coin's inscription again. It was an ancient Hebrew text, an obscure reference to a pivotal moment in the history of Israeli intelligence. This wasn't random violence; this was something far darker, far more calculated. As he examined the inscription, a chilling realization began to take root. There was a sinister connection tying together the seemingly unrelated elements of the case— the murders, the Israeli mob, the coin, Miriam's mysterious past, and the shadow of the Mossad.

Pickens knew, with a certainty that ran deep to his bones, that this was just the beginning of a far more complex and terrifying game. What had begun as an investigation was now a fight for survival, one that stretched far beyond the confines of his detective work. He wasn't just playing to close a case anymore—he was playing for his life.

Converging Paths

The rain hammered relentlessly against the corrugated iron roof of the abandoned warehouse, its harsh percussion blending with the rhythmic thud of Pickens's boots as they echoed on the cold concrete floor. The air was thick with the metallic scent of blood and the sickly sweet stench of decay. He knelt beside the body, another Pakistani cab driver—the fourth in as many weeks.

The same chilling precision. The same absence of struggle. The same methodical efficiency. This was no random spree; it was a targeted execution.

Pickens studied the scene with a practiced eye, missing nothing. The faint scent of expensive cologne lingered in the air, a stark contradiction to the grime of the warehouse. He noted the body's careful placement, the almost artistic arrangement of scattered possessions. This was a statement, a taunt, a deliberate act of defiance. This wasn't merely murder; it was theater.

His hand moved instinctively to the victim's pocket, retrieving the familiar object—a tarnished silver coin, identical to the one found at the previous crime scenes. The ancient Hebrew inscription remained a cryptic enigma, a puzzle piece in a game he was only beginning to comprehend. The coin, a relic of a forgotten era, spoke of a history cloaked in secrecy—one that connected these seemingly random killings to something far larger, far more sinister.

Pickens's phone buzzed, yanking him from his thoughts. It was Miriam. He hesitated, then answered. Her voice, usually bright and vibrant, trembled with fear. "Tommy, it's happening again," she whispered, her words barely audible above the noise of the city. "They're after me."

Pickens's gut clenched. He'd suspected a connection between Miriam and these murders, a suspicion now solidified by the eerie similarities between the victims' profiles and the people Cohen had crossed in his dark past. The fragmented clues he had gathered were beginning to coalesce into a terrifyingly clear picture. Cohen. It had to be Cohen.

He raced to Miriam's apartment, the wail of his patrol car's siren a desperate counterpoint to the pounding of his heart. He found her trembling, eyes wide with terror, a crimson stain blooming across the silk of her blouse. She hadn't been attacked, but she had seen something—someone. A shadow lurking in the alleyway, a fleeting glimpse of a cruelly handsome face she recognized all too well.

Pickens knew he was chasing a ghost—a specter from Miriam's past, a past twisted inextricably with the brutal present. He had to find Cohen, not only to solve the murders but to protect Miriam, the woman who had become enmeshed in the dangerous tapestry of his investigation. The lines between duty and personal involvement were blurring, threatening to consume him.

His investigation led him down a rabbit hole, a labyrinth of secret meetings, shadowy figures, and coded messages. He delved deeper into Cohen's world—a world built on betrayal, violence, and unspeakable cruelty. Pickens uncovered Cohen's history, his ties to the Israeli mob, his cold efficiency, his utter lack of remorse. The trail of bloodshed stretched across Morocco, where Cohen had honed his lethal skills, leaving a wake of broken bodies and shattered lives.

He learned of Cohen's expulsion from Mossad, the fallout from a failed operation, and the dark secret buried beneath layers of official deniability. He pieced together Cohen's motivations—resentment simmering toward the Israeli government, bitterness fueling his descent into a life of crime. The murders weren't random; they were meticulously planned acts of revenge, a vendetta against those Cohen believed had wronged him.

Pickens discovered that the victims, though seemingly unrelated, all had one thing in common: each had ties to the operation that had led to Cohen's downfall. Each murder was a message—a chilling demonstration of Cohen's calculated brutality. He wasn't just killing; he was sending a warning.

The investigation led Pickens into the heart of the Israeli mob, a shadowy network of ruthless criminals operating beneath the surface of New York City. He navigated the perilous waters of organized crime, relying on his instincts and cunning to survive. He walked a tightrope, balancing his investigation against the constant threat of betrayal and violence.

He encountered informants, double-crossers, and players with loyalties on both sides. He learned to trust no one, to question everything, and to rely only on his own judgment. He found himself caught in a web of deception, where the truth was obscured by layers of lies, and where the lines between friend and foe blurred more each day.

The deeper he dug, the more he realized this was no ordinary murder investigation. It was a conspiracy—one that reached far beyond the city's boundaries and into the corridors of power and influence. He uncovered a plot involving individuals at the highest levels of government and intelligence.

The investigation brought him face-to-face with the ghosts of Cohen's past, the echoes of his brutal actions reverberating through the city's underworld. Pickens found himself staring into the abyss, the terrifying realization that he was playing a deadly game against a master strategist—someone who was always several steps ahead of him.

The pressure mounted. The clock was ticking. He had to find Cohen before Cohen found him. The stakes had never been higher. His life, Miriam's life, and perhaps even the stability of the city itself hung in the balance. The converging paths of Pickens's investigation and Cohen's criminal enterprise were headed for a collision, a confrontation that would determine not only the fate of the city but their own. Pickens was no longer just a detective chasing a series of murders—he was a pawn in a deadly game, one played with lives and destinies. And the final move was about to be made.

A Dangerous Liaison

The flickering neon sign of a nearby bar cast a lurid glow across the rain-slicked street, illuminating Miriam's anxious face as she watched Pickens's squad car disappear around the corner. She hadn't told him everything—not by a long shot. The truth, a tangled web of betrayal and bloodshed spun by Sharon Cohen, was far too dangerous to reveal so freely. She had given Pickens just enough to keep him invested, enough to fuel his investigation, but she had carefully guarded the most damaging details—the ones that could implicate her, that could expose her own dark and dangerous past.

The gnawing fear in her gut was a constant companion these days. Cohen's shadow stretched long and dark across her life, a chilling reminder of the violence he was capable of. She had escaped his clutches once, but she knew he wouldn't rest until he had his revenge. And now, Pickens, with his unwavering gaze and relentless pursuit of justice, had unwittingly become a pawn in Cohen's twisted game. Their relationship, born from shared grief and a mutual respect for the law, was now a dangerous liaison—a delicate tightrope walk above a chasm of violence.

The thought of Cohen discovering her connection to Pickens sent a shiver down her spine. He was ruthless, efficient, and possessed an unnerving ability to anticipate his enemies' every move. He had once been her lover, her confidante, but now he was a predator, stalking her from the shadows. The memories of their time together—the shared secrets and whispered promises—were now tainted by the bitter taste of betrayal and the chilling echo of his violence. The man she had known was gone, replaced by a monster driven by vengeance and fueled by a thirst for power.

She had known Cohen before he became the shadowy figure he was now. She had witnessed his transformation—the slow erosion of his morality as his disillusionment with Mossad festered and grew. His descent into the criminal underworld hadn't been a sudden plunge; it had been a gradual, insidious slide, each transgression paving the way for the next. She had tried to help him, to pull him back from the abyss, but her efforts had been futile. Her pleas had fallen on deaf ears, her warnings dismissed as the naive ramblings of a woman out of her depth.

Now, she found herself trapped in a web of her own making. She had used Pickens, leveraging his investigation to protect herself, but in doing so, she had put him in grave danger. She knew Cohen wouldn't hesitate to eliminate anyone who stood in his way, and Pickens, in his relentless pursuit of justice, had become a significant obstacle. The weight of her actions pressed down on her, a suffocating burden of guilt and fear.

Pickens, meanwhile, remained blissfully oblivious to the danger that lurked just beneath the surface of his budding relationship with Miriam. He was captivated by her intelligence, her resilience, and the faint mystery that clung to her like a second skin. He saw her as a strong woman, a survivor—someone who deserved his protection. He hadn't connected the dots. He hadn't realized the significance of the cryptic clues she had offered, the half-truths and carefully constructed omissions that had slipped from her lips.

He was consumed by the case, the relentless pursuit of the killer leaving little room for reflection or introspection. Nights blurred into mornings as he poured over files, analyzed crime scene photos, and chased down dead-end leads. Each new victim added another layer of complexity to the investigation, pushing him closer to the edge of madness.

The city, once his familiar hunting ground, now felt like a labyrinth—an ever-shifting maze of shadows and secrets, where the line between right and wrong had become dangerously blurred.

He found himself drawn to Miriam's strength, her quiet determination. She offered an escape from the grim reality of his work, a fleeting refuge from the pressure and the unending cycle of violence that consumed him. He had hoped that their relationship might provide some semblance of normalcy in his chaotic life. But the deeper he got involved with her, the closer he was pulled into the heart of the darkness that enveloped Cohen's criminal empire.

What he didn't yet understand was that the string of murders—seemingly random—was part of a larger, far more sinister plan. The Pakistani cab drivers, the wealthy Israeli businessmen, were not just victims. They were carefully chosen targets, each elimination serving a specific, deadly purpose in Cohen's grand scheme. Pickens had yet to grasp the full scope of Cohen's machinations: an elaborate web of deceit and manipulation stretching across continents, tying together players in a deadly game of power and revenge.

Unbeknownst to Pickens, Cohen was watching him— meticulously tracking his every move. He had sensed the developing relationship between Pickens and Miriam and knew it presented a significant threat to his operations. Cohen had to eliminate Pickens, but he wouldn't resort to a simple, direct confrontation. A master manipulator, Cohen preferred to work in the shadows, pulling strings from afar.

His plan was devious, involving Miriam as a pawn in his game. He would exploit her connection to Pickens, drawing him into a trap. He would prey on her vulnerabilities—her lingering feelings for him, her fear of his wrath. Through subtle manipulation, he would coax her into making mistakes, revealing key information that would lead Pickens straight into a dangerous ambush. Miriam would be the key to Pickens's demise.

The rain continued its steady fall, a somber soundtrack to the unfolding drama. The city slept, oblivious to the deadly game playing out in its dark corners. Pickens, unaware, was chasing shadows, walking unknowingly toward a confrontation that would test his skills, his resilience, and his very life. He was a pawn in a much larger game, a game controlled by a strategist always several steps ahead. And at the center of it all, trapped between two dangerous men, was Miriam—her fate hanging by a thread.

The stakes were rising, the danger intensifying with every passing moment. The lives of Pickens and Miriam had become inextricably intertwined with Cohen's criminal empire. Their fates were now bound to his ultimate downfall. The collision was inevitable, the confrontation imminent. The city held its breath, unaware of the storm brewing in its shadows. The truth behind the web of lies and deceit remained veiled, waiting to be revealed.

And all the while, the ticking clock of Cohen's plan counted down—the metronome of violence, each second bringing them closer to a violent, decisive clash.

Targets of Opportunity

The desert wind, hot and unforgiving, lashed at Cohen's tailored suit as he surveyed the opulent villa from across the manicured lawn. Every detail of this target had been meticulously chosen. Avraham Ben-Zvi, a diamond magnate with deep ties to the Israeli underworld, was known not only for his extravagant wealth but also for his unyielding security. But Cohen thrived on challenges, and Ben-Zvi's layers of protection were no match for his expertise. Already, two security barriers had been bypassed, using a blend of bribery and brutal efficiency—his signature style. Tonight, the target wasn't just Ben-Zvi's wealth; it was the satisfaction of dismantling another pillar of the establishment he so despised. Cohen had tasted betrayal, felt the sting of injustice, and now, he dispensed his own brand of twisted justice.

The cold weight of his silenced pistol against his thigh brought a sense of reassurance.

For weeks, Cohen had studied Ben-Zvi's every move, mapping his routines, learning his weaknesses. The man's arrogance had become his undoing. He'd grown complacent, believing himself untouchable. Cohen couldn't help but smirk at the thought. The hunt, the calculated risk, the thrill of outwitting his prey—these were what truly exhilarated him. In the dark, he was a phantom, a whisper in the shadows, a predator stalking his chosen victim.

The villa's security was state-of-the-art, but Cohen had anticipated this. Days ago, he'd exploited a weakness in the network's firewall, a chink in the armor that even Ben-Zvi's expert security team had overlooked. Moving with the silent grace of a desert cat, Cohen bypassed infrared sensors, disabled motion detectors, and neutralized the guard dogs with a precisely timed tranquilizer.

He found Ben-Zvi in his study, surrounded by stacks of cash. The man's face glowed in the soft light of a monitor displaying real-time market fluctuations. Ben-Zvi looked up, startled, as Cohen materialized in the doorway—a silhouette against the moonlight. The terror in Ben-Zvi's eyes was unmistakable. He reached for the alarm button on his desk, but Cohen was too fast. A single, sharp shot echoed through the still room, followed by the sickening thud of a body hitting the plush carpet.

Cohen examined his work, a grim satisfaction twisting his lips. He wiped the weapon clean, meticulously removing any trace of his presence. He left no witnesses, no fingerprints, no clues. He was a ghost, leaving only a chilling void in his wake.

The next target was a stark contrast. No high walls or luxury, just a cramped, dimly lit taxi depot in the rundown section of Queens. This wasn't a carefully planned operation—it was a spur-of-the-moment decision, fueled by a sudden surge of rage. The Pakistani cab drivers, Cohen had learned, were tangled in a lucrative smuggling ring, operating under the radar of both law enforcement and the Israeli mob. In his twisted morality, Cohen saw them as collateral damage in a much larger game.

He chose his victim at random—Salim Khan, a middle-aged driver, weary from years of hard labor. Khan was counting his earnings when Cohen appeared. Before the man could react, Cohen's fist landed with brutal force, sending him crashing to the ground. The attack wasn't clean, calculated, or precise. It was raw, fueled by primal rage, a break from the cold calculation Cohen usually embodied.

Khan groaned, his breath muffled by the thick carpet as Cohen rifled through his pockets, snatching the cash. He left the depot quickly, blending into the anonymity of the night. But the act left him cold—an unsettling reminder of how far he had fallen. The thrill of the game was fading, replaced by an emptiness that gnawed at him. He was becoming the very thing he despised—a cold-blooded killer, operating outside the law and morality.

The killing of Khan marked a shift. It lacked the calculated precision of his earlier acts. It was impulsive, brutal, a sign of his unchecked rage and self-loathing. This new, savage violence was an escalation, signaling his own moral decay. The city, a sprawling labyrinth of shadows, was now his hunting ground, his playground.

His next assignment, however, was different—a far more sophisticated task. This wasn't personal vengeance or the thrill of the hunt; it was business, pure and simple. A lucrative contract to eliminate an element within the Muslim Brotherhood, a man suspected of infiltrating the U.S. government. The contact, a shadowy figure known only as "The Serpent," had reached Cohen through a network of intermediaries. The details were vague, encrypted in secrecy, but the price was right—enough to fund a lavish escape to a secluded island paradise, far from the violence and betrayal that had consumed his life.

This was a task requiring meticulous planning—surgical precision, not brute force or impulsive violence. Cohen spent weeks researching Mahmoud al-Fadil, a charismatic leader with global connections. He studied al-Fadil's routines, security protocols, and vulnerabilities. He infiltrated al-Fadil's inner circle, using charm, deception, and intimidation to gain trust. He learned everything about his target—his family, his friends, his fears—and turned al-Fadil's own people against him.

Cohen's expertise went beyond violence. He was a master of manipulation, deception, and psychological warfare. Fluent in multiple languages, he could disappear into a crowd, blend with the shadows, and become invisible when needed.

The operation to eliminate al-Fadil was a masterpiece of espionage. Cohen orchestrated the death to look like a tragic accident, a mishap that left no trace of foul play. Authorities believed it was simply a misfortune, unaware of the complex web of manipulation Cohen had spun. When it was over, Cohen vanished, leaving only the chilling remnants of his efficiency.

But the city never forgets. The shadows have long memories.

As Cohen disappeared into the global underworld, a new threat emerged—a relentless detective, closing in on his trail. His past, the tangled web of lies and betrayal, was unraveling. The game was far from over. The shadows were closing in, and the city was waiting. Sharon Cohen, the ghost, knew his time was running out. The price for his freedom was about to come due. The weight of his actions pressed down on him—guilt and fear suffocating him—but there was no turning back. Trapped in an inescapable cycle of violence, Cohen had become a predator in his own shadow, with nowhere to run. What had once been exhilarating now felt like a desperate struggle for survival.

The Brotherhood Contract

The desert air hung thick and heavy, carrying the scent of jasmine mingled with something metallic, faintly sickening. Cohen adjusted the silk scarf around his neck, the fine fabric a stark contrast to the rough-hewn stone of the Marrakech riad where he awaited his contact. He had been in Morocco for months now, a chameleon shifting between identities, each more shadowy than the last. The Israeli mob had provided a comfortable, albeit morally reprehensible, existence. But this... this was different.

His contact, a wiry man named Omar, arrived precisely at midnight. His eyes carried the weight of ancient wisdom and the cynical sharpness of a lifetime spent navigating the treacherous undercurrents of the criminal world. He offered Cohen mint tea, its sweetness a deceptive contrast to the bitterness of the deal that was about to unfold.

"The Brotherhood," Omar began, his voice a low rasp, "is concerned about a leak. A rat in their ranks, ambitious and reckless. He believes he can manipulate the system, gain influence within the American government. A naive fool, but a dangerous one nonetheless."

Cohen, sipping his tea, remained silent. He had expected details, but Omar's words were deliberately vague—a reflection of the Brotherhood's legendary secrecy and their deep mistrust of outsiders, even those like Cohen who thrived in the murk of the shadows. He had learned to read between the lines, to decipher unspoken words, the subtle gestures that betrayed a man's true intentions. Omar's evasion, however, intrigued him. It hinted at a deeper layer of conspiracy, a hidden agenda that both fascinated and unnerved him.

"This man… What's his name?" Cohen finally asked, his voice low and controlled.

Omar hesitated, then leaned in closer, his breath hot against Cohen's cheek. "His name is… not important. His actions are. He's already made contact with several high-ranking officials, attempting to offer… information, let's say." He paused, letting the weight of the unspoken implications hang in the air. "The Brotherhood wants him silenced. Permanently."

Cohen considered this. The Muslim Brotherhood wasn't a monolithic entity; factions and rivalries abounded, each vying for power. A rogue element attempting to infiltrate the U.S. government posed a serious threat to the established order— one that could unravel years of carefully constructed networks and influence. This wasn't a simple assassination; it was a strategic operation, a high-stakes move on a global chessboard.

"And the compensation?" Cohen inquired, his gaze unwavering.

Omar smiled, a chilling flash of white teeth against tanned skin. "More than you'd make in a year working for the Israeli mob. And more importantly, access. Access to things you can't even imagine."

The implications were tantalizing. The access Omar offered could reshape Cohen's life, give him the leverage to settle old scores, to dismantle the system that had betrayed him. It was a dangerous game, but one Cohen thrived in.

"Tell me everything," Cohen said, the icy glint in his eyes reflecting the moonlight filtering through the riad's courtyard.

Over the next few hours, Omar laid out the details. The target, he revealed, was a man named Dr. Tariq Khalil, a charismatic yet ruthless figure who had rapidly risen through the ranks of the Brotherhood. Khalil possessed sensitive and potentially explosive information, capable of triggering political turmoil on both sides of the Atlantic. He operated under the guise of an academic, lecturing at prestigious universities, subtly weaving his way into circles of power. His cover was impeccable; his network, extensive. Eliminating him would require finesse, precision, and, above all, anonymity.

The contract was audacious—an operation of high stakes that spoke to Cohen's innate thirst for danger. It was a dance with death, a game of cat and mouse played out in the shadowy alleys of Washington, D.C., a far cry from the sun-drenched streets of Marrakech.

The following weeks were a blur of meticulous planning. Cohen tapped into his network to gather intelligence on Khalil. He studied Khalil's routine, movements, and associates, piecing together a puzzle that demanded both cunning and brutality. He analyzed satellite imagery, surveillance footage, even Khalil's social media activity, searching for weaknesses, for opportunities.

He assembled a team—a shadow crew of specialists: a former intelligence officer with expertise in counter-surveillance, a master forger, and a tech expert capable of breaching the most advanced security systems. They were ghosts, operating in the gray areas of legality, their skills honed by years spent in the shadows. Their loyalty was bought, not earned, tied to promises of vast sums of money and the thrill of a dangerous game.

Cohen spent hours studying the layout of Khalil's Washington, D.C. apartment—an opulent penthouse overlooking the Potomac River. He knew the security would be tight, but he was prepared. A master of infiltration, capable of bypassing sophisticated systems with ease, Cohen crafted a multi-layered operation that demanded flawless execution.

The night of the operation arrived, shrouded in a cold November rain. Cohen's team, cloaked in darkness, moved with the precision of a well-oiled machine. They disabled security cameras, bypassed motion sensors, and slipped past guards like phantoms. Cohen himself, dressed in a tailored suit that blended seamlessly with the night, used his charm and ruthlessness to navigate the remaining security checkpoints—intimidation and well-placed bribes working in tandem.

He found Khalil in his study, surrounded by stacks of papers and flickering computer screens. The academic looked up, surprised but not panicked. He had known, on some level, that the shadows were closing in. The knowledge only fueled Cohen's resolve.

The encounter was swift, efficient, almost clinical. A silenced weapon, a quick strike, and Khalil collapsed onto his expensive Persian rug, his blood staining the plush fibers. Cohen's team cleaned the scene with eerie precision, erasing all traces of their presence. They vanished as quickly and silently as they had arrived, leaving behind only the silence of the night and the lingering scent of rain.

Back in his Marrakech riad, Cohen counted the money—substantial sums neatly packaged in a worn leather briefcase. But it wasn't just the money that mattered. It was the knowledge that he had just played a high-stakes game with global implications. A game that had left him standing tall, menacing in the shadows—a testament to his resilience and unmatched skills. The city might remember, but it wouldn't be able to connect him to Khalil's death—not yet.

His past, however, was a ticking time bomb, ready to explode at any moment. It threatened to unveil his dark and clandestine history. The shadows of his past would eventually catch up with him, but for now, he reveled in his temporary victory. The game, he knew, was far from over.

The Wiretap

The crackle of static punctuated the otherwise silent room. Detective Tommy Pickens leaned forward, his eyes fixed on the monitor, where the waveform of a tapped phone line danced in rhythm with his heartbeat. Weeks of painstaking surveillance, countless dead ends, and the gnawing frustration of chasing shadows were finally yielding results. The target: Miriam Elbaz, a former Mossad operative and Sharon Cohen's ex-lover. The bait: a seemingly innocuous phone call with the potential to unravel a web of deceit, murder, and international espionage.

The voice on the recording was unmistakably Miriam's—brittle, hesitant, her fear cutting through even the electronic distortion. "Sharon," she whispered, her voice barely audible over the hum of the city. "They're closing in. Pickens...he's onto something."

Pickens felt a surge of adrenaline. He knew Miriam—her sharp intelligence, her unyielding resolve. The fear in her voice was genuine, chilling. And the mention of his name? A direct hit to his ego, a validation of his relentless pursuit. He'd been hunting Cohen like a phantom, a shadow slipping through the underbelly of New York, leaving a trail of bodies and broken lives. Now, he had a lead—a real, tangible lead.

The conversation continued, fragmented at first, but slowly it began to reveal a picture more disturbing than Pickens could have imagined. Cohen, in his characteristically arrogant yet cautious tone, dismissed Miriam's concerns. "Relax, sweetheart," he sneered, his voice a low growl, laced with forced calm. "They're amateurs. I've dealt with worse. Much worse."

The conversation veered, shifting into cryptic references to Morocco, a hidden stash of something valuable, and impending threats. Pickens scribbled furiously in his notepad, trying to decode the language, the half-truths, and veiled warnings. Mentions of "the Brotherhood" caught his attention—a term linked to the Muslim Brotherhood's covert network—and a vague threat about "someone in Washington." The pieces began to fall into place, revealing a conspiracy far more grandiose and dangerous than he'd ever suspected.

The conversation ended abruptly, leaving Pickens with more questions than answers. But the wiretap had given him something vital: confirmation of Cohen's presence in the city, a tangible link to the string of murders he was investigating. He was no longer chasing shadows. He had a name, a location, and a motive, though still hazy.

He replayed the tape multiple times, meticulously noting every nuance—the inflections, the pauses, the subtle changes in tone. He could hear the desperation in Miriam's voice, the underlying current of fear she struggled to hide. He knew she loved Cohen, despite his brutal betrayal, despite the violent assault that had left her scarred both physically and emotionally. That loyalty—flawed and dangerous—could be the key to breaking Cohen.

The next step was securing Miriam's cooperation. It was a delicate maneuver, a risky gamble. Cohen was dangerous, unpredictable, and would stop at nothing to protect himself. Turning Miriam against him could prove fatal—for her, and for Pickens. He had to tread carefully, earn her trust, convince her he wasn't just another hunter closing in for the kill.

Pickens knew he couldn't approach Miriam directly. He needed a subtle approach, an indirect line of communication. So, he enlisted the help of a contact within the Israeli consulate, a seasoned diplomat who had dealt with Mossad operatives before. They needed someone Miriam trusted, someone who could reach her without alerting Cohen.

Days turned into weeks, and the investigation deepened. Pickens' team tirelessly traced Cohen's movements through surveillance footage, financial records, and phone logs. They were closing in, but Cohen proved to be a slippery adversary, a master of deception. His trail was littered with false leads, airtight alibis, and an unnerving absence of tangible evidence.

The pressure mounted. The Mayor's office was breathing down his neck, demanding results. The media painted the city as a powder keg, teetering on the brink of chaos. Pickens knew he was playing a high-stakes game—a game where one wrong move could cost him everything.

Then, a breakthrough. A confidential informant, a low-level member of the Israeli mob operating in Brooklyn, provided crucial intel about a meeting between Cohen and a shadowy figure known only as "The Broker." This individual, rumored to have ties to the Muslim Brotherhood, was said to be involved in a large sum of money changing hands—a high-value transaction, possibly linked to the contract Cohen had accepted.

The meeting location: a secluded warehouse on the docks. It was a high-risk play, a gamble Pickens couldn't afford to ignore. Fueled by a mixture of righteous anger and professional ambition, he mobilized his team, coordinating a multi-pronged operation. SWAT teams surrounded the warehouse, snipers stationed on rooftops, while undercover officers infiltrated the area. Pickens and a small team were tasked with leading the assault, capturing Cohen alive if possible.

The operation unfolded with precision, Cohen and The Broker ensnared in the law enforcement net. But as the raid progressed, a shocking twist revealed itself. The Broker turned out to be a high-ranking Mossad official, secretly working with Cohen, orchestrating events from the shadows. The Muslim Brotherhood contract? A smokescreen—a diversion for something far more sinister: a plan to destabilize the U.S. government through a series of covertly orchestrated events.

Chaos erupted. Cohen, armed and defiant, fought back fiercely, his years of training and experience enabling him to evade capture. He was a blur of motion, a phantom slipping through the smoke and turmoil of the warehouse. The gunfight was deafening, the air thick with gunpowder and fear.

In the aftermath, several officers were injured. The Broker was apprehended, but the trail leading to the heart of the conspiracy remained elusive. Cohen, however, was gone, vanishing into the labyrinth of Brooklyn's streets. Pickens's frustration was palpable, the sting of defeat bitter on his tongue. He had underestimated Cohen's cunning, his ruthlessness, his ability to slip through the cracks. But that defeat only fueled his determination. He would not rest until Cohen was brought to justice.

The wiretap had provided the initial breakthrough, but it hadn't delivered the decisive blow. It had revealed a deeper conspiracy—a betrayal within Mossad, a shadow war playing out on a global stage. And it had only stoked Pickens's relentless pursuit of Sharon Cohen, the ghost he vowed to hunt down at any cost. The game, far from over, had just entered a more dangerous phase.

Miriams Dilemma

The fluorescent hum of the interrogation room contrasted sharply with the storm brewing inside Miriam Elbaz. Her reflection, pale and drawn, stared back from the polished steel table, the harsh light accentuating the shadows under her eyes—testaments to countless sleepless nights spent wrestling with her conscience. Detective Pickens, a man whose quiet intensity could melt steel, sat opposite her, his gaze unwavering. He wasn't cruel, not overtly, but his silence was a pressure cooker, building tension that threatened to explode.

He hadn't pressed her hard, not at first. He understood the value of patience, the subtle art of coaxing the truth from a fractured soul. He had extended a lifeline, a deal amidst the storm of her betrayal. Testify against Cohen, help dismantle his network, and he would ensure her safety, a new identity—a chance to escape the shadow of her past. It was a tempting offer, a siren's song promising a life free from violence, the chilling memories of betrayal.

But Miriam's loyalty to Cohen, twisted and perverse as it was, clung to her heart like a stubborn knot. It wasn't love, not anymore. It was something darker, a warped sense of kinship forged in the fires of shared secrets and clandestine operations. They were two sides of the same coin, both scarred by the brutal realities of espionage, both haunted by ghosts they could never outrun. Even his violent assault on her, the shattering of her trust, couldn't entirely erase the bond they once shared. It had warped it, yes, made it toxic—but it hadn't broken it entirely.

Her silence had endured for days, punctuated only by the occasional sigh, a nervous twitch of her hand—the subtle betrayals of her body language. Pickens had laid out the evidence—wiretaps, intercepted communications, eyewitness accounts—painting a grim portrait of Cohen's descent into depravity. He spoke of the victims, the lives shattered by Cohen's ruthlessness, the destruction left in his wake. He showed her pictures: the bruised face of a Pakistani cab driver, the opulent apartment of a targeted Israeli businessman, the bullet-riddled walls of a Moroccan safe house.

Each piece of evidence hammered another nail into Cohen's coffin, each blow striking Miriam's already fragile composure. The weight of her complicity pressed down on her, the knowledge that she had unwittingly aided Cohen in his horrific acts. She had been blind to his descent, her loyalty blinding her to the monstrous transformation overtaking the man she once loved. The revelation was crushing, leaving her spiraling in a vortex of self-recrimination and regret.

The memories flooded back: their training together at Mossad, the thrill of clandestine operations, the camaraderie amidst danger. She recalled the chilling efficiency of Cohen's methods, the ruthless pragmatism that allowed him to compartmentalize his actions, to justify his violence in the name of a greater cause. Now, stripped of that illusion, those actions were revealed for what they truly were—acts of pure malevolence.

She had tried to rationalize it, to convince herself that Cohen was still acting out of a twisted sense of justice, a warped ideology he clung to after his betrayal by Mossad. But the evidence shattered that delusion. This wasn't about justice; it was about power, greed, and the intoxicating allure of unchecked brutality. The man she knew had vanished, replaced by a monster consumed by his own demons.

Pickens understood her hesitation. He saw the internal battle raging within her, the tug-of-war between fear and loyalty, between self-preservation and the lingering vestiges of a broken bond. He didn't push; he simply waited, letting the weight of the evidence speak for itself. He let her see the faces of the victims, let her glimpse the full extent of Cohen's cruelty. He knew that the most effective weapon in his arsenal wasn't intimidation, but the slow, agonizing erosion of her defenses.

He knew, too, that there was more to it than just Cohen. There was a deeper conspiracy hinted at in the wiretaps, shadows lurking behind Cohen's actions, whispers of betrayal within the highest echelons of power. The information Miriam held could be the key to unraveling it all, a key that could lead to a network far larger, far more dangerous than Cohen himself. The stakes extended far beyond the streets of New York, reaching into the dark corners of international espionage and political intrigue.

The silence stretched on, broken only by the rhythmic tick-tock of the clock on the wall, a relentless reminder of time slipping away. Miriam stared at her hands, her knuckles white as she clenched and unclenched her fists. She thought of her family, the life she had once envisioned, a life that Cohen had stolen from her—a life she could regain if she chose to cooperate.

The thought of Cohen's wrath, should she betray him, sent a shiver down her spine. His ruthlessness was legendary. He had silenced many before, eliminating threats with chilling efficiency. But the fear of his retribution was fading, overshadowed by the growing awareness of her own culpability. She had allowed herself to be blinded by a warped sense of loyalty, a loyalty that had made her complicit in his crimes.

She closed her eyes, picturing Cohen's face—the cruel glint in his eyes, the chilling indifference to the suffering he caused.

Then she thought of the victims, of the innocent lives destroyed by his actions, the families left shattered by his ruthlessness. The image of the Pakistani cab driver's son, clutching a tattered photograph of his father, was particularly potent. The boy's face, etched with grief and despair, became a mirror reflecting Miriam's internal struggle.

The weight of her silence suddenly became unbearable. The fragile edifice of her loyalty to Cohen crumbled, dissolving into the dust of guilt and remorse. With a shudder, she opened her eyes, her gaze locking with Pickens'. The decision had been made. The floodgates opened. The dam of her silence finally broke. The game had changed. And it wouldn't be long before the full weight of Miriam's testimony shattered the web Cohen had woven around them all.

The chilling realization dawned on her: revealing the truth was just the beginning of a far more dangerous journey. A journey into the heart of a conspiracy that could shake the foundations of governments and expose the hidden corruption at the very highest levels of power. The web, she realized, was far larger, far more complex than she could have ever imagined.

Pickenss Pursuit

T he precinct felt colder than usual that night. The fluorescent lights hummed like angry wasps, a fitting soundtrack to the icy dread that had settled in Pickens' gut. Miriam's confession had been a dam bursting, a torrent of information flooding over him, leaving him breathless and reeling. He'd known Cohen was dangerous, a viper coiled in the shadows, but the extent of his depravity—the reach of his criminal network—far surpassed anything Pickens had anticipated. Cohen wasn't just dealing drugs or robbing banks; he was operating on a scale that threatened to unravel the very fabric of international security.

The details Miriam had provided were chillingly specific: coded messages, offshore accounts, names whispered in hushed tones—names of powerful figures in Israeli politics, shadowy figures in the Muslim Brotherhood, and even rumors of a connection to someone within the upper echelons of the U.S. government. What had begun as a simple murder case had morphed into a hydra-headed beast, its tentacles reaching into the darkest corners of the globe.

Pickens felt the weight of the world on his shoulders, the responsibility of untangling this complex web of deceit and violence. He was no longer just a detective; he was a soldier in a silent war, fighting an enemy far more formidable than he'd ever imagined.

He stared at the map spread across his desk, a patchwork of locations spanning three continents. Morocco, where Cohen had spent years operating within the Israeli mafia, was a starting point. Then there was New York, where the recent murders had occurred, followed by Washington D.C., where whispers of Muslim Brotherhood infiltration grew louder. Each pin on the map represented a potential lead, a fragment of the puzzle that needed to be pieced together. The thought of failing, of letting Cohen escape, sent a jolt of adrenaline through him. He wouldn't let that happen. He couldn't.

His phone buzzed, pulling him back from his thoughts. It was his contact in Morocco, a grizzled veteran of the local police force, a man who owed Pickens a considerable debt of gratitude from a past operation. "Pickens," the voice rasped through the speaker, "we found something. A warehouse on the outskirts of Casablanca. It's not flashy, but the activity there... it's consistent with Cohen's MO."

The warehouse. A potential goldmine of evidence. Pickens felt a surge of renewed purpose. He assembled his team—a small, handpicked group of seasoned detectives and intelligence analysts. He briefed them on the information Miriam had provided, emphasizing the need for discretion and precision. This wasn't just a run-of-the-mill drug bust; they were dealing with a highly organized criminal network with international ties. One wrong move could blow their cover and alert Cohen.

The flight to Casablanca was long and tense. Pickens replayed Miriam's testimony in his mind, dissecting every detail, every nuance. Her fear had been palpable, but beneath it lay a steely resolve, a determination to see Cohen brought to justice. He owed it to her, to the victims, to the city, to the country—to bring him down. He had to.

The Casablanca warehouse was a grim, dilapidated structure nestled among a labyrinth of dusty alleys and crumbling buildings. The air was thick with the scent of salt and decay. Under the cover of darkness, Pickens and his team moved in, their movements precise and silent, like shadows in the night.

They secured the perimeter, setting up surveillance equipment and establishing a communication network.

The raid itself was swift and brutal. The warehouse proved to be a treasure trove of evidence: weapons, encrypted communications devices, financial records, and a list of names that would send shivers down the spines of even the most hardened intelligence officers. Among the documents, Pickens found a ledger detailing Cohen's transactions—a meticulous record of his dealings with various criminal organizations around the globe. The sheer volume of information was overwhelming, a testament to Cohen's intricate and far-reaching criminal enterprise.

But the biggest shock came when they discovered a hidden room behind a false wall. Inside, they found a single battered laptop. Its hard drive, however, contained something far more significant than financial records. It contained Cohen's personal files—a detailed chronicle of his descent from a Mossad agent to a ruthless criminal mastermind. Pickens felt a chill crawl down his spine as he read the chilling details, each sentence a testament to the man's arrogance and cold-blooded ruthlessness.

The laptop contained information about the Al-Qaeda bombing, Cohen's role in it, and the subsequent removal of gold reserves from the World Trade Center. The documents confirmed the depth of Cohen's betrayal of his country, his descent into the dark abyss of criminal activity. There were coded messages hinting at even more dangerous plots—plots that reached into the highest echelons of power.

As the sun rose over Casablanca, casting long shadows across the dusty streets, Pickens felt a grim satisfaction. They had dealt a crippling blow to Cohen's criminal network, dismantling his operation and gathering irrefutable evidence. But it was far from over. Cohen was still out there—a ghost in the machine, his web extending to places Pickens had never imagined. He would be relentless in his pursuit, determined to bring the man down, even if it meant uncovering secrets that could shatter governments and expose a conspiracy threatening the very fabric of global security. The investigation had only just begun. The web, he knew, was far from unraveled.

The flight back to New York was filled with the quiet hum of anticipation. Pickens knew the information he possessed was explosive, a ticking time bomb waiting to detonate. He had to proceed cautiously, carefully navigating the treacherous currents of international politics and organized crime. He had to protect his sources, protect himself, and protect the city from the fallout of what he had uncovered.

Back in his office, the map remained spread across the desk, now adorned with more pins, each one representing a new lead, a new threat, a new challenge. The pursuit of Sharon Cohen had become a mission—a crusade to bring down a criminal mastermind whose web of deceit reached into the highest levels of power. The path ahead was fraught with danger, but Pickens was ready. He was prepared to face whatever lay ahead, prepared to fight for justice—even if it meant confronting forces far greater than himself. The game was far from over. The fight had just begun. And Detective Pickens, armed with the chilling truth, was ready to face the storm.

Mossads Shadowy Interest

The grainy image on Pickens' monitor flickered, casting an eerie glow as a shadowy figure emerged from the labyrinthine alleys of a Marrakech souk. The pixelated quality was deliberate, a digital veil designed to obscure the finer details, but even through the distortion, Pickens recognized the swagger, the near-imperceptible limp—Sharon Cohen. The image was timestamped three days prior, just before the violent attack on a Pakistani cab driver, a seemingly random act that, in light of Miriam's revelations, now felt chillingly deliberate. It wasn't random; it was a message. A warning, perhaps, or a threat. The question was, to whom?

Miriam had spoken of Cohen's shadowy connections, of his whispered double-dealings, and of his tendency to sell information to the highest bidder. He had always been a loose cannon, but now, it seemed, his trajectory was purposefully erratic, almost as if it were designed to mislead. This wasn't just a rogue agent gone astray; it was a carefully orchestrated performance—a theater of chaos staged for an unseen audience. And that audience, Pickens suspected, was far more powerful than any criminal syndicate.

He leaned back in his chair, the stale air of the precinct clinging to him like a suffocating shroud. The Moroccan footage was but one piece of the puzzle, a shard reflecting a far larger, more sinister picture. His investigation had tunneled beneath the surface of organized crime, uncovering a vast and intricate network that spanned continents and reached into the highest echelons of international power. Cohen was a pawn, yes, but a pawn of immense value—the kind that could easily ascend to the role of a kingmaker.

Pickens picked up the latest intelligence report, a thick dossier detailing Cohen's financial transactions. The scale of the money laundering was staggering—shell corporations, offshore accounts, and a dizzying array of complex financial instruments. The trail led to Geneva, Zurich, the Cayman Islands—familiar hotspots in the world of high-stakes laundering. But there were anomalies, subtle discrepancies that hinted at something far more sophisticated, something pointing toward state-sponsored activity.

The report mentioned encrypted communications intercepted between Cohen and various unknown parties. The messages, while heavily coded, were frequent and urgent, suggesting something monumental was at play. Pickens had passed the intercepts to the NSA, but their response had been frustratingly vague—"under review." The lack of urgency spoke volumes. This wasn't about drug trafficking or contract killings; this was something far larger, something that reached into the highest levels of government.

Pickens' gut told him that Mossad was involved—not necessarily in orchestrating Cohen's crimes, but in monitoring them, perhaps even manipulating them to serve their own agenda. Cohen's initial betrayal of Mossad, his subsequent descent into the underworld—it all felt too convenient, too perfectly timed. It was as if Cohen's actions were being orchestrated, a choreographed dance of chaos designed to serve a larger, unseen purpose. Was Mossad using Cohen as a tool to destabilize elements within the Middle East, a deliberate diversion to draw attention away from their own covert operations?

The timing of the Al-Qaeda bombing plot and the removal of Israeli gold reserves from the World Trade Center struck

Pickens as too precise, too calculated, suggesting inside knowledge and impeccable planning. Cohen's infiltration of Al-Qaeda was the key. But why would the Israeli government allow such a potentially devastating event to unfold, even if they stood to profit from it? It seemed reckless—almost suicidal. Unless, of course, it was all a carefully calculated risk, a necessary sacrifice to achieve a greater strategic objective.

And what was that objective? Was it to eliminate a rival faction within Al-Qaeda? To divert attention from a different operation? Or was it something even more sinister? The possibilities were endless, each more unsettling than the last. The entire situation reeked of a double-cross, a global-scale deception, and Cohen—violent, betraying Cohen—was the perfect patsy, the ideal scapegoat.

He reached for the phone, his fingers hovering over the digits. This was a long shot, a desperate gamble, but he had to try. He needed someone who understood the intricacies of Middle Eastern geopolitics, someone who could unravel the threads of this complex web.

The call connected to a CIA contact, a seasoned analyst with an unparalleled grasp of Mossad's operations. "I need some help," Pickens began, his voice low and urgent.

He outlined his suspicions, presenting the evidence he'd gathered—painting a portrait of Cohen as a double agent, a puppet manipulated by unseen forces. The analyst listened intently, his silence thick with years spent navigating the treacherous waters of international espionage.

The conversation unfolded into hours of analysis—decoding messages, tracing financial transactions, discussing the shadowy world of global intelligence. As the conversation progressed, it became clear that Pickens' suspicions weren't unfounded. There were indeed signs of Mossad's involvement—not in orchestrating Cohen's crimes but in using his actions to their advantage. The gold reserves and the timed bombing plot now made sense—a calculated risk to protect their assets and advance their strategic goals.

The analyst agreed that Cohen's seemingly random acts of violence could, in fact, be deliberate attempts to create chaos, to mislead investigators and obscure his true activities. The attacks on Pakistani cab drivers and wealthy Israelis—all fit into a pattern, a carefully constructed charade designed to protect the interests of a far more powerful entity. He cautioned Pickens to proceed with extreme caution. This wasn't a simple criminal; this was the deep state at play.

The call ended with a chilling revelation. The analyst disclosed that Cohen's file within Mossad contained classified information that had been redacted—too sensitive to be released even to high-ranking officials. This missing information, the analyst speculated, held the key to understanding Cohen's true motives and his ties to Mossad's clandestine operations. It was a clear indication that Cohen's actions were part of a far larger, highly classified operation, one that reached into the highest echelons of power. Pickens felt a chill run through him. The implications were staggering. He was no longer chasing a criminal; he was hunting a ghost, a phantom controlled by forces far beyond his understanding.

As he hung up the phone, the weight of the situation pressed heavily upon him. This case was no longer about capturing a criminal; it was about unraveling a conspiracy that reached the very top of global power. The seemingly random acts of violence, the money laundering, the encrypted communications—each was a piece of a meticulously crafted puzzle, designed to conceal a far darker truth. The web tightened, woven from deception, betrayal, and international intrigue that threatened to consume him. And somewhere out there, Sharon Cohen—the pawn—was playing his part, perhaps unaware of the game's true stakes, or perhaps, all too aware, playing a role far more dangerous than he could ever imagine. The fight had just begun, and Pickens knew he was in way over his head.

Closing the Net

The scorching Moroccan sun beat down on Cohen's rented villa, the heat suffocating, a thick blanket smothering the already humid air. He had traded the precision of Mossad for the chaotic desperation of the underworld—a descent he once reveled in, but now found himself suffocating under. The thrill had long since faded, replaced by an unshakable unease, a sense of being watched, a nagging feeling that the intricate web he had woven was beginning to unravel.

His phone buzzed, slicing through the oppressive silence like an unwelcome intrusion. A burner, of course—a disposable number he swapped every few days. It was a precaution he had learned the hard way. The voice on the other end rasped, thick with a Castilian accent.

"Señor Cohen," the voice hissed. "There's been a... complication."

Complications were Cohen's specialty, a constant thread in the tapestry of his life. Yet this felt different, the usual casual menace now sharpened with urgency. "What kind of complication?" he asked, his voice unsettlingly calm, though a prickling sensation crept along the back of his neck.

"The Americans," the voice rasped. "They're getting closer. Much closer than we anticipated."

The Americans. Pickens. The thought sent a chill of dread through Cohen. He hadn't anticipated the relentless pursuit of the NYPD detective, whose dogged tenacity had become a thing of nightmare. Pickens wasn't just after a common criminal; he was hunting a ghost, a phantom who moved through the murky depths of the international criminal underworld. And now, Cohen realized, he was closing in, tugging at the loose threads, tightening the noose around him.

Cohen's mind raced, quickly piecing together the scattered fragments of information. The Pakistani cab driver, Miriam's assault—these weren't random acts. They were breadcrumbs, carelessly discarded by a man desperate to maintain control. He had underestimated Pickens' intellect, his uncanny ability to connect even the most seemingly unrelated dots.

The complication, Cohen realized, wasn't merely Pickens. It was the convergence of multiple forces—Mossad, the Israeli mob, the American branch of the Muslim Brotherhood, and now, the ever-present U.S. intelligence agencies. Each force pulled in a different direction, each with its own motives, creating a violent maelstrom of intrigue that threatened to swallow him whole.

He needed to disappear. Fade back into the shadows, but where could he go? His past was a persistent ghost, every step tracked, every connection scrutinized. Morocco, once his sanctuary, was now rapidly becoming a prison.

The following days blurred into frantic activity. Cohen bounced between increasingly dilapidated and insecure safe houses, burning burner phones, shredding documents, erasing every trace of his existence. He felt like a hunted animal, each step taken with the weight of his sins pressing on his chest.

Omar, his money-laundering contact—an unscrupulous, overweight businessman—had begun to crack. Omar, usually a paragon of discretion, was now visibly on edge, fretting over the increasing scrutiny from both Moroccan and American authorities. His anxiety, though irritating, was yet another sign. The net was tightening.

One evening, nursing a lukewarm mint tea in a dimly lit café in Marrakech, Cohen noticed a familiar figure across the square. It wasn't Pickens, but it might as well have been. A gaunt, shadowy figure, the unmistakable silhouette of someone Cohen knew from his days with Mossad. He was known only as "The Falcon." A legend, a ghost story among Mossad agents, a man feared for his ruthlessness and efficiency. His presence here, in this forgotten corner of Morocco, sent a shiver down Cohen's spine.

The Falcon's cold, calculating gaze locked onto Cohen's, no greeting, no pleasantries—just a silent acknowledgment, a chilling reminder that even in the darkest corners of the world, some operated beyond shadows, beyond the reach of even the most cunning criminals.

Cohen knew immediately what this meant. Mossad was cleaning house. They were eliminating loose ends, ensuring no one could untangle the web of deception they had so carefully woven. He had become an inconvenient truth, an obstacle to be eradicated.

The realization struck him like a physical blow. He wasn't just being hunted by the NYPD; he was now a target of Mossad, the very organization he had once served with unshakable loyalty. His betrayal had left him exposed, vulnerable—a pawn in a far larger game.

Desperation surged through Cohen as he fled the café, tearing through the labyrinthine alleyways of the medina. The Falcon's presence was the final confirmation of his worst fears. He wasn't just up against Pickens and the American authorities;

he was facing Mossad—the full, cold-blooded might of an organization notorious for its efficiency, ruthlessness, and its complete disregard for human life.

The chase that followed was brutal—a desperate fight for survival. Cohen, driven by adrenaline and fear, used his knowledge of the city's hidden passages and his ingrained survival instincts to stay one step ahead of his pursuers. But the Falcon and his team were relentless, their pursuit clinical, calculating. He was being hunted, every move anticipated.

For days, Cohen evaded capture, relying on his cunning, his knowledge of Marrakech's underbelly, and the network of contacts he had built over years as both an operative and a criminal. But the city—once his refuge—had become a prison, its narrow streets and winding alleys offering little respite from the pursuit.

His supplies dwindled, his body worn thin by sleep deprivation, the constant strain of evading his captors. The toll was taking its toll. Cohen knew he was losing the battle of attrition, and the end was inevitable.

Trapped in a decaying building overlooking the ancient ramparts of Marrakech, Cohen heard the approaching footsteps echo in his ears. The net, woven from lies, betrayal, and years of calculated risks, had finally closed in on him. He raised his weapon, a bitter smile tugging at the corners of his lips. The end had come. It was as brutal and unforgiving as the life he had chosen to lead.

The fight was over, but the consequences of his actions would reverberate long after his death. The web, once his creation, had become his inescapable prison—a tangled mess of espionage, crime, and deceit. His life—an intricate mosaic of lies and betrayals—was about to be reduced to a single, tragic point.

A Desperate Gamble

The stale air of the interrogation room hung heavy, thick with the scent of cheap disinfectant and unspoken desperation. The fluorescent lights buzzed, a relentless counterpoint to the frantic rhythm of Sharon Cohen's pounding heart. He was trapped, cornered like a rat in a maze, the walls closing in with the relentless efficiency of a well-oiled machine. But Cohen wasn't your average rat. He was a viper—venomous, unpredictable, and unwilling to go down without a fight.

His capture had been chaotic, a ballet of gunfire and shattered glass—a testament to his stubborn refusal to surrender. Even now, despite the handcuffs biting into his wrists, a flicker of defiance burned in his eyes. He had underestimated the NYPD's tenacity, underestimated Detective Pickens's obsession, and most importantly, he'd underestimated the reach of his own past. The wiretap on Miriam's phone had been his undoing, a betrayal he hadn't seen coming, a blind spot in his meticulously constructed world of deceit.

But the game wasn't over. Not yet. Cohen had spent years navigating the treacherous currents of the Middle East, outwitting Mossad, manipulating the Israeli mob, and even playing both sides against the middle with the Muslim Brotherhood. Escape was a gamble, a desperate throw of the dice—but it was one Cohen was willing to take. His life, after all, had been a series of high-stakes gambles, each one more reckless than the last.

His plan was audacious, bordering on insane. It hinged on a network of contacts he'd cultivated over the years—a patchwork of loyalties and grudges, alliances forged in the fires of betrayal and cemented with blood. First, he needed to reach his contact within the Moroccan prison system—Omar, a hulking brute and former soldier with a penchant for violence and a price for his silence. Omar held the key to the outside: a network of smugglers and corrupt officials who could whisk Cohen away into the anonymity of the souks.

Getting a message to Omar wouldn't be easy. The prison was heavily guarded, the surveillance relentless. But Cohen had a plan. He'd use his limited interactions with other inmates to subtly pass along the message, relying on a coded system only Omar would understand. It was a dangerous dance—a slow burn of anticipation—every conversation a potential risk, every glance a calculated move.

The days crawled by, each one a testament to Cohen's patience and resilience. He feigned compliance, played the part of the defeated spy, all the while orchestrating his escape. He befriended a small-time thief, a wiry man named Khalil, offering him protection in exchange for a small service: the delivery of a hidden message. Khalil, ever opportunistic, readily agreed. Cohen trusted no one—least of all Khalil—but the man was a necessary cog in his machine, a disposable piece in the intricate game of chess he was playing.

The message reached Omar. The response came in the form of a subtle gesture—a stolen cigarette, a whispered word during a routine prison check. The escape was on. The plan was intricate, involving a staged riot, a carefully timed diversion, and a daring climb over a section of the prison wall notorious for its weak mortar.

The night of the escape was shrouded in darkness, the air thick with tension. The riot broke out with surprising ferocity, a whirlwind of shouting men and flailing limbs. Amid the chaos,

Cohen and Khalil slipped away, unnoticed in the melee. The climb was treacherous, the drop perilous—but Cohen, fueled by adrenaline and desperation, made it over the wall, landing hard on the other side. Freedom, at last, was within his grasp.

But freedom was a fleeting illusion, a mirage in the desert of his life. Omar's network wasn't as impenetrable as he'd claimed. Pickens was one step behind, his dogged determination a relentless shadow, fueled by both professional duty and a personal vendetta. Miriam's testimony, though reluctant, had painted a vivid picture of Cohen's brutality, adding another layer of complexity to the investigation.

Cohen found himself running—fugitive in his own country, pursued by the law and haunted by his past. He was a ghost, a specter in the labyrinth of Morocco, forever looking over his shoulder, forever dodging the long arm of the law. His escape had been a desperate gamble, a reckless act of defiance—but it had only prolonged the inevitable. The game, it seemed, was far from over. The betrayal ran deeper than he'd ever imagined. Mossad, it turned out, hadn't completely abandoned him. They were playing their own game, using him as a pawn in a larger geopolitical chess match. The lines between friend and foe, ally and adversary, blurred into an indistinguishable haze.

His erstwhile allies, members of the Moroccan underworld, were beginning to question his loyalty, sensing his desperation. The money promised for his escape dwindled, replaced by threats and demands. He was now caught in a crossfire—a pawn in a deadly game he didn't fully understand, manipulated by forces beyond his comprehension. He had been betrayed—not only by Miriam but by the very people he thought he could trust.

The escape had bought him time, a precious commodity in the world of espionage, but it hadn't solved his problems. It had only compounded them. He was alone, hunted, and betrayed, with nowhere to turn. His past had caught up with him—not just in the form of the relentless Detective Pickens, but in the form of his own choices, the consequences of his actions echoing through the dusty alleys of Marrakech. The final act of this brutal drama was yet to unfold—a bloody showdown that would determine his fate and possibly the fate of others. The game was far from over. The desert sands held the secrets of his past, the ghosts of his betrayals, whispering warnings in the hot wind. He was running out of time, out of options, and out of hope. The only thing he had left was his cunning, his ruthlessness, and the burning desire to survive. He'd gamble it all, one last time. This time, the stakes were higher than ever. This time, failure meant more than just capture—it meant death.

Unexpected Alliances

The desert wind lashed sand against Cohen's face, stinging his eyes as he navigated the winding alleys of Marrakech. His escape from the police had been a chaotic ballet of gunfire and near-misses, a testament to his honed instincts and years spent evading capture. But freedom was a fragile thing, a fleeting illusion in the harsh reality of his situation. He was still hunted, his past a relentless shadow dogging his every step. He needed help—and he needed it fast.

His mind raced, sifting through the debris of his fractured life, searching for a lifeline. He thought of the Israeli mob, the brutal men he'd once worked alongside—men who spoke the language of violence and betrayal. They were snakes, yes, but snakes could be useful, especially when cornered. Reaching out to them felt like swallowing poison, but survival demanded bitter choices.

His first contact was a hulking man named Yaakov, a veteran of countless underworld wars. Yaakov responded to Cohen's coded message with a curt, "Show up at the usual place. I have something to discuss. Don't bring trouble." The usual place was a dimly lit, smoke-filled backroom of a Marrakech casino, the air thick with the stench of stale beer and desperation.

The meeting was tense—a silent battle of wills between two men who knew the depths of darkness all too well. Yaakov listened impassively to Cohen's desperate plea for aid, his expression unreadable behind dark sunglasses. The request was audacious, bordering on suicidal: Cohen needed safe passage out of Morocco, a network of contacts to help him disappear, and enough money to start anew, far from the long arm of the law and the vengeful wrath of Detective Pickens. In exchange, Cohen offered Yaakov a tempting quid pro quo: information about a lucrative arms deal involving a rogue faction within the Moroccan army.

Yaakov considered the offer, his gaze fixed on Cohen's hardened face. "You're a ghost, Cohen," he finally said, his voice gravelly. "A ghost that's become a liability. But the arms deal... that's juicy. I can use that. But trust? That's a luxury we can't afford."

The uneasy alliance was forged in mutual need, sealed by an unspoken understanding of the brutal rules of the game.

Yaakov, however, insisted on collateral. Cohen had to provide proof of his claim—detailed dossiers on the arms deal, names, dates, locations—everything. It was a risk, revealing vital information to a man he could hardly trust, but Cohen had no choice. His survival hinged on the success of this dangerous gamble.

His next move was even more perilous. He had to reach out to someone he had betrayed—someone with every reason to want him dead: Miriam, his former girlfriend. He'd brutally assaulted her, shattering not only her physical well-being but also her trust. Reaching out to her now, asking for help, was an act of desperation, a gamble that could easily backfire.

He found her in a small, unassuming apartment in Casablanca, guarded by a fierce-looking bodyguard. The years had etched lines of worry into her face, but her eyes still held a spark of defiance. She listened in silence as he laid out his desperate situation, his words carefully chosen—a plea wrapped in a cloak of manipulation. He offered no apologies, no remorse. He only offered an opportunity: revenge against the man who had orchestrated his downfall, Detective Pickens. The offer was a poisonous cocktail of self-preservation and vengeance, but it was enough to sway her.

The alliance with Miriam was fraught with tension, a silent acknowledgment of their shared history of betrayal and violence. But their mutual hatred for Pickens, and their knowledge of his methods, formed a fragile bridge of shared purpose. Miriam possessed invaluable information about Pickens' investigation, contacts within the NYPD, and the intimate details of his life. Cohen realized this knowledge could be their ticket to freedom, a chance to outmaneuver their common enemy.

The alliance between Cohen, Yaakov, and Miriam was a bizarre tapestry woven from threads of mutual self-interest, betrayal, and vengeance. It was an unlikely coalition, a pact forged in desperation and propelled by the shared desire to survive. Their collective skills and knowledge formed a formidable force, a counter-offensive against the forces arrayed against them. The coming confrontation would be a brutal chess match, where the stakes were life and death, and every move carried the potential for catastrophic failure.

As he prepared for the final showdown, Cohen knew this wasn't merely a fight for survival; it was a reckoning. A confrontation not just with Pickens, but with the ghosts of his past—the consequences of his choices, the weight of his betrayals. His escape route, meticulously crafted with the help of his unlikely allies, would lead him through a labyrinth of deceit and danger, demanding cunning, nerves of steel, and unwavering determination to survive.

He met Yaakov again, this time in a secluded desert oasis. The silence was broken only by the rustling of palm leaves and the distant cry of a hawk. Yaakov provided Cohen with forged documents, a new identity, and a route out of Morocco—a clandestine network that spanned across the Sahara Desert into the heart of West Africa. The arms deal information had already been passed on to Yaakov's contacts, and the flow of money had begun.

Meanwhile, Miriam had infiltrated Pickens' circle, feeding him misinformation and planting seeds of doubt. She was playing a dangerous game, one that could expose her at any moment, but her hatred for Pickens outweighed her fear. She knew he was closing in, that Cohen's escape was only a matter of time before he tracked him down. Her contribution to Cohen's escape was vital. The information she relayed was crucial to outwitting Pickens' tracking efforts.

The escape plan was complex—carefully choreographed movements and diversions. Cohen, using his new identity and forged documents, would travel through a network of hidden routes, assisted by Yaakov's men. Miriam, operating from within Pickens' circle, would provide real-time updates on the detective's movements, allowing Cohen to anticipate his next move and stay one step ahead.

Their final meeting before the escape was tense. They stood in the shadows, three figures bound together by circumstance and a shared desire for revenge. There was no trust, only a grim understanding of their mutual survival. As Cohen prepared to leave, Miriam handed him a small, worn photograph. It was a picture of her and Cohen, taken years ago—before the betrayal, before the violence, before their lives spiraled out of control. It was a haunting reminder of what they had lost, a symbol of their fractured past.

The desert night swallowed Cohen whole as he embarked on his dangerous journey. His escape was far from guaranteed—a treacherous path fraught with peril and uncertainty. But he had his allies, however unlikely, and their shared purpose fueled his resolve. The game was far from over. The final act had yet to unfold, but Cohen, armed with his cunning, ruthlessness, and the ghosts of his past, was ready to play. He was a viper—and he would strike again.

Double Crosses and Deception

The flickering gaslight cast long shadows as Cohen met his contact, a wiry man named Omar, in a dimly lit Marrakech souk. Omar, a former member of the Moroccan intelligence service with a penchant for backstabbing, was Cohen's only link to a potential escape route—a hidden passage through the Atlas Mountains leading to a network of smugglers operating along the Algerian border. The price for passage was steep, not just in dirhams, but in loyalty. Omar, eyes gleaming with avarice, laid out his terms—a carefully constructed web of deceit designed to entrap Cohen further. He wanted information—sensitive intelligence on Cohen's past dealings with Mossad, details that could fetch a king's ransom on the black market.

Cohen, his face a mask of practiced nonchalance, listened patiently. He knew Omar was playing a dangerous game. Their meeting wasn't a straightforward transaction; it was a dance of suspicion and calculated risk. He'd anticipated this, preparing for the need for a counterplay. He'd already planted a seed of doubt in Omar's mind, feeding him misinformation about a fictitious cache of weapons hidden somewhere in the old medina. This was a diversion, a tactic to buy himself time.

"I can give you what you want, Omar," Cohen said, his voice a low rumble. "But I need assurances. You know how these things work. Betrayal is a costly business." He paused, letting the words hang heavy in the air, the unspoken threat a palpable presence between them.

Omar chuckled, a dry, rasping sound. "Of course, my friend. Trust is a luxury we can't afford. But I assure you, this will be a mutually beneficial arrangement. The information you provide will ensure your safe passage. Failure to cooperate... well, let's just say the mountains are full of hungry wolves."

The next few days were a blur of clandestine meetings, whispered conversations, and carefully orchestrated exchanges. Cohen fed Omar carefully crafted lies, a carefully constructed tapestry of misinformation that would hopefully expose the man's duplicity. He strategically leaked a few fragments of truth—enough to keep Omar hooked but not enough to compromise his own safety. Meanwhile, he was quietly making preparations for his own escape, contacting a separate network of contacts—individuals he trusted implicitly, unlike the treacherous Omar. He'd played the double-cross long enough to anticipate Omar's own strategy. He was being played, but he was also playing the game back.

This double-crossing strategy, however, came at a cost. As Cohen's deception deepened, the stakes grew higher. He received a cryptic message from his former handler in Mossad, a man named Avram, offering him a chance to redeem himself—an opportunity to use his unique skills to help Israeli intelligence thwart an imminent attack. The proposition was laced with veiled threats and thinly disguised manipulation. Avram, it seemed, still held a powerful leverage over Cohen. It was a classic Mossad maneuver, a subtle attempt to lure him back into their web of intrigue. Cohen understood the tactic— this was a dangerous game of cat and mouse, where a wrong move could be fatal.

Cohen knew that accepting Avram's offer would mean aligning himself with Mossad once more—a step that went against his very core. He had tasted freedom, however fleeting, and the thought of returning to the suffocating embrace of the Israeli intelligence apparatus filled him with a sense of dread. But he also understood the consequences of refusal. Avram held the power to unleash a torrent of information that could ruin Cohen's chances of escaping Morocco forever.

This presented a dilemma. He considered his options: trusting Avram and returning to the fold, a path laden with risk and the potential for more betrayals; rejecting Avram and facing the consequences of his defiance, leaving him vulnerable to both Mossad and Omar. He was caught in a web of conflicting loyalties, a prisoner of his past actions. He was facing a double-cross of epic proportions.

Meanwhile, Detective Pickens, in New York, was closing in on Cohen. His investigation into the string of murders and robberies had led him to a series of seemingly unrelated events—the theft of gold reserves from the World Trade Center, the subsequent bombing, and now, the trail of victims in Marrakech. Pickens's investigation, driven by his relentless pursuit of justice, began to reveal a network of international crime, a clandestine world where Israeli mobsters, Al-Qaeda operatives, and rogue intelligence agents collided. He was uncovering Cohen's tracks, closing the net.

Pickens's relationship with Miriam, Cohen's former girlfriend, was also growing complicated. Miriam, haunted by her past with Cohen and fearful for her own safety, was struggling to come to terms with the depth of Cohen's deceit and betrayal. She hesitated about providing Pickens with the full picture of Cohen's involvement, fearing the repercussions if Cohen found out. But the detective's persistence started chipping away at her defenses. The constant threat hanging over her head began to win over her hesitation.

Unbeknownst to Pickens, Miriam was secretly communicating with Avram, feeding him information on Cohen's whereabouts.

This was a desperate attempt to secure her own safety, but it also represented a significant betrayal of both Cohen and Pickens. Miriam's actions were a desperate bid for survival—a silent plea for protection in a world where alliances shifted as quickly as the desert sands.

She was playing her own game of survival, and the stakes were just as high for her.

As the net tightened around Cohen, he realized that the game was not simply about escaping from Omar or evading Pickens. It was about surviving the intricate web of deception he had spun—a web that was now ensnaring him. The double-crosses he had orchestrated were backfiring, creating a cascade of betrayals that threatened to consume him. He found himself in a deadly game where every move was a gamble, and the odds were stacked against him. His escape was no longer a simple matter of survival; it was now a war for his very life. He had to outwit not just Omar and Pickens, but also Avram and Miriam. This was his final battle—a desperate fight for survival in a world where trust was a luxury he could no longer afford. The fight for survival was now a complex war of attrition, a battle of wits between multiple players, each with their own agenda and motives.

A Bloody Showdown

The desert wind whipped around Cohen, stinging his eyes as he scrambled across the jagged terrain. Omar's men were hot on his heels, their guttural shouts echoing through the canyons. He had underestimated Omar, the viper's betrayal sharper than any blade. The hidden passage, the promised escape route, had been nothing more than a cruel joke in the face of impending death. Cohen had known Omar was treacherous, but the depth of his deceit had blindsided him. The information Omar had demanded—details of Cohen's Mossad operations, his dealings with the Israeli mob—wasn't merely to secure passage; it had been bait, expertly designed to lure him into a trap.

He'd managed to escape the initial ambush, a hail of bullets whistling past his head, but his injuries were slowing him down. His leg, grazed by a stray bullet, throbbed with agonizing pain, each step a fresh wave of torment. He cursed his arrogance, his overconfidence. He had survived countless dangerous missions, outwitted seasoned professionals, yet he'd been blindsided by a man whose cunning was as brutal as his greed.

The moon cast long, distorted shadows, making the already treacherous landscape even more perilous. Cohen stumbled, his breath ragged, his body screaming in protest. He needed cover, a moment to regroup, to plan his next move. Then, he saw it—a narrow crevice in the rock face, just wide enough to squeeze through. It offered a sliver of protection, a temporary respite from the relentless pursuit.

He limped into the crevice, the cool stone a welcome relief from the scorching desert heat. He pulled out his first aid kit, tending to his wound as best he could. The pain was intense, but adrenaline masked the severity of his injury. He knew he couldn't afford to linger here. Omar wouldn't relent. He needed a plan, a way out of this deadly game.

His mind raced through his options. Fighting his way out was suicide with his leg injured and being outnumbered. Surrendering was unthinkable—Omar would torture him, extract every last bit of information, and then kill him anyway. There was only one choice left: turn the tables, use his cunning to outwit his pursuers.

Then it came to him—an underground cave system, a labyrinthine network of tunnels only known to a few. A smuggler had once whispered of it. If he could find it, he might have a chance.

He rose, gritting his teeth against the pain, and set off again with newfound resolve. He moved cautiously, every rustle of leaves, every snap of a twig sending a jolt of fear through him. He was playing a deadly game of cat and mouse—and this time, he was the mouse.

As he neared the cave entrance, he saw them—Omar and his men, silhouetted against the moonlight. They were closing in, their faces grim, weapons drawn. This was it—the final showdown. Cohen steeled himself, ready to fight for his life.

The ensuing firefight was brutal, a chaotic ballet of bullets and screams. Despite his injury, Cohen fought with the ferocity of a cornered animal. He used the terrain to his advantage, weaving through the rocks, using the shadows for cover. He took down several of Omar's men, but they were relentless, their numbers overwhelming.

Then one of Omar's men—a hulking brute with a scarred face—charged at him, a wicked curved dagger gleaming in the moonlight. Cohen dodged the first strike, but the man's strength was overwhelming, his attacks unyielding. In a desperate move, Cohen grabbed the man's arm, twisting it until he heard a sickening crack. The man screamed, dropping his dagger. Cohen seized the opportunity, yanking the dagger from the ground and plunging it deep into the brute's chest.

But the fight was far from over. Omar, his face contorted with rage, advanced on him, a pistol in his hand. Cohen knew he was outmatched, outnumbered. He had already exceeded his expectations—he'd hoped for a clean break, a simple escape from his past. But this wasn't an escape. This was a bloody battle for survival.

As Omar raised his weapon, a gunshot rang out from behind him. Omar spun around, his eyes widening in shock. Miriam. Her face pale, a pistol smoking in her hand. She had found him. She had tracked him across the unforgiving desert. She had come to save him—but why?

The betrayal ran deeper than he ever imagined. Miriam, the woman he had betrayed, assaulted—the woman he had once believed to be his enemy—was now his unlikely savior. But her motives were unclear, shrouded in darkness as deep as his own. Her presence shifted the balance of power, complicating matters in ways he hadn't anticipated. Had she come to save him, or to finish him off? Was this another layer of deceit in the twisted web of betrayal? Her eyes, though filled with concern, held a coldness that hinted at a hidden agenda.

The remaining members of Omar's gang hesitated, momentarily stunned by Miriam's unexpected appearance. Cohen seized the opportunity. He launched himself at Omar, tackling him to the ground. They grappled in the dust, a fierce struggle for dominance. Fueled by adrenaline and the desperate will to survive, Cohen managed to overpower Omar, disarming him and delivering a crushing blow to his head. Omar crumpled, unconscious. His reign of terror was finally over.

But the night wasn't over yet. As the remaining members of Omar's gang scattered into the shadows, another figure emerged—Detective Pickens. His face grim, weapon drawn. He had been tracking Cohen, following the trail of violence and betrayal. He'd seen the confrontation from a distance, his silent observation adding another layer of tension to the already tangled situation.

The sight of Pickens filled Cohen with a wave of despair. His escape, his survival, now seemed impossible. Trapped between the woman he had hurt and the detective determined to bring him to justice, Cohen realized he had played his cards, outwitted enemies, and manipulated situations to his advantage—but this? This was a game he couldn't win.

As Pickens approached, Miriam stepped in front of Cohen, shielding him with her body. The tension in the air was thick, heavy with unspoken words, with betrayal, and with the lingering scent of gunpowder and desert dust. The final showdown wasn't over—it had simply shifted focus. The players were caught in a macabre dance of vengeance and redemption. The desert night held its breath, waiting for the next move, the next betrayal, the next act in this tragic drama.

The desert itself seemed to hold its breath, a silent witness to the unfolding story, a canvas on which the brutal brushstrokes of fate were being painted. And Cohen, battered and bleeding, knew this was far from the end. This was merely the beginning of a new chapter, a deeper layer of deceit and danger, in a game where the stakes were impossibly high. Every move was a gamble, and the odds were hopelessly stacked against him. His survival now depended not only on his wits but on the unpredictable whims of fate—and the hidden motives of the people around him. He had underestimated his enemies, his allies, and even himself. In this unforgiving desert, this lethal cocktail of uncertainty could easily be his undoing. The night was far from over.

The Price of Betrayal

The flickering gaslight cast long, distorted shadows across the dusty interrogation room. Cohen, his face a roadmap of bruises and cuts, sat hunched in a chair, the rough-spun fabric digging into his aching flesh. He had expected pain, had braced himself for the brutal interrogation tactics of Omar's men, but the gnawing emptiness inside him was far more agonizing than any physical torment. The betrayal of Omar, his supposed ally, had left a wound deeper than any bullet. He had sacrificed everything—his loyalty, his identity, his very soul—for a promise that had crumbled to dust in the unforgiving desert.

The interrogator, a hulking figure with eyes like chips of obsidian, leaned closer, his breath hot and rancid on Cohen's face. "The names, Cohen. Give us the names. We know you were working with others." His words were a low growl, a threat laced with the chilling promise of more pain. Cohen remained silent, his gaze fixed on a crack in the wall, his mind a whirlwind of fractured memories and agonizing regrets.

His descent into darkness had been gradual, almost imperceptible at first. The disillusionment following his Mossad operation, the sting of betrayal by his own government, had pushed him toward the fringes, to the shadowy corners where morality blurred and survival became the only rule. The Israeli mob in Morocco had offered him a twisted sense of belonging, a haven of violence and deceit. The drugs, the money, the power—they had all been temporary distractions, fleeting moments of oblivion in a life drowning in regret. Miriam, his former lover, had been a victim of this descent, a casualty in his brutal game. He had traded his soul for a life of fleeting pleasures, and now, the price was coming due.

He thought of Miriam—her face, once radiant with laughter, now haunted by fear and pain. The memory of her betrayal, the way she had sacrificed his own information to buy her own safety, echoed in his mind like a death knell. The memory of his violent act against her lingered, sharp and unforgiving. He had justified it then, as a necessary evil in the brutal chess game he played. Now, looking back, it was nothing short of monstrous. He had betrayed her trust—and the trust of the people he once swore to protect. The weight of it all threatened to crush him.

The interrogator's hand tightened on his shoulder, a sharp dig into the bone. "The Muslim Brotherhood contact," he hissed. "The one you were supposed to eliminate. Give us his name, and maybe we'll spare you some pain."

Cohen's mind raced. He had taken the contract solely to secure more resources—another step down the path of self-destruction. The Muslim Brotherhood contact, a man named Khalil, was a phantom, a ghost in the shadows of Washington D.C. Revealing Khalil's identity would betray not only his own code, but could unleash disastrous global consequences. But in this grim reality, silence was a luxury he could no longer afford.

The interrogator's voice was ice cold. "Silence only prolongs the inevitable, Cohen. We know everything. We have your past, your present, and we can easily predict your future. We know about the Moroccan operation, the gold, Miriam. It's all right here." He slapped a file onto the table, the weight of it a heavy thud in the otherwise silent room.

Cohen hesitated. The cost of silence versus the cost of betrayal hung precariously in the balance. The pain, the brutality, it all felt inconsequential. It was the moral abyss he now found himself drowning in that truly chilled him to the core. He had betrayed so many. How much more could he bear to lose?

With a sigh, heavy with resignation and despair, he began to speak. The floodgates opened, releasing a torrent of details, names, locations, and dates. Each word was a fresh stab of self-loathing. Each confession a surrender to the inescapable reality of his fate. The intricate web of lies he had spun, the alliances forged in deceit, began to unravel, thread by thread.

He spoke of his time with Mossad, painting a grim picture of institutional corruption and moral compromises. He spoke of his descent into the criminal underworld, the intoxicating allure of power and wealth, the brutal realities of betrayal and violence. He spoke of Omar, of the desert betrayal, of the promise of escape that turned into a death trap. He spoke of the victims—innocents whose lives had been extinguished in a brutal dance of power. He confessed to every crime, laying bare the sordid details, leaving nothing unsaid.

The interrogator listened, his expression unreadable. His eyes never left Cohen's, piercing through the facade of hardened defiance, exposing the fractured soul beneath. The confession went on, a torturous odyssey through a life lived in shadows, a narrative of unchecked ambition, moral compromise, and the ultimate price of betrayal.

When Cohen finished, a heavy silence settled over the room. The only sound was the rhythmic tick-tock of a clock, a relentless reminder of time's passage, and the irreversible damage he had inflicted. The interrogator stood, his shadow stretching across the floor like a specter of justice.

"We knew most of it, Cohen," he said, his voice devoid of emotion. "But this... this is more satisfying than we anticipated." He paused, his gaze piercing. "You've played your last hand."

The weight of his confessions settled upon him like a suffocating blanket of guilt. It wasn't just the physical pain that wracked his body, but the profound agony of his soul. The desert wind, the sting of betrayal, the harsh realities of the Moroccan underworld—these were mere precursors to the torment he now faced. He had traded his soul for fleeting pleasures, and now, the price was being exacted. Justice, cold and final, was being meted out in the unforgiving light of consequence. The game was over. He had lost.

As he looked into the cold, emotionless eyes of his interrogator, he realized that there was no redemption, only a bleak, desolate future awaiting him. The price of betrayal, he now understood, was far higher than he had ever imagined.

The Hunt Continues

The biting New York wind whipped around Detective Tommy Pickens as he stared out at the churning gray expanse of the East River. The city, usually a vibrant tapestry of noise and light, felt muted tonight, a reflection of the gnawing emptiness inside him. Sharon Cohen's arrest had been a victory, a hard-fought win against a man who seemed to exist in a perpetual twilight zone between shadow and light. But the victory tasted like ash. The case, far from closed, felt like a Gordian knot, its threads tangled in a web of international intrigue and personal betrayal.

Miriam's testimony, while crucial, had only scratched the surface. She'd confirmed Cohen's involvement in the string of murders, painting a chilling portrait of a man consumed by rage and fueled by a deep-seated sense of betrayal. She'd spoken of his brutal efficiency, his cold calculation, and his chilling lack of remorse. But she'd also revealed glimpses of the man he once was—the idealistic Mossad agent who'd been shattered by the events surrounding the World Trade Center bombing and the subsequent abandonment by his superiors.

That man, Miriam implied, was still lurking beneath the hardened criminal. The question was, could he ever be reached?

Pickens ran a hand through his already disheveled hair. The sheer scale of Cohen's operation was staggering. The murders, the drug trafficking, the contract on the Muslim Brotherhood operative—all pointed to a meticulously planned network, one that extended far beyond Cohen himself. He'd been a pawn, a highly skilled and deadly pawn, but a pawn nonetheless. The question that haunted Pickens was, who was pulling the strings?

The investigation had stalled. Cohen, despite his capture, remained tight-lipped. He'd offered a defiant smirk and a chillingly calm silence in the face of interrogation. His lawyers, a formidable team of high-powered attorneys, were already spinning elaborate defenses, painting him as a victim of circumstance, a man pushed to the brink by betrayal and corruption.

Pickens knew this wasn't the end. He felt it in the hollow ache in his gut, in the persistent knot of unease that refused to loosen its grip. Cohen's network was too vast, too intricate, to have simply vanished with his arrest. There were loose ends, unanswered questions, whispers in the shadows that suggested a larger conspiracy, one that reached into the highest echelons of power.

He pulled out the file, the worn pages a testament to the countless hours he'd spent poring over the details of the case. The details of the World Trade Center gold were still a mystery. The official explanation—a coincidence, a tragic accident—rang hollow in Pickens's ears. Cohen's actions suggested a deeper link, a connection that seemed inextricably tied to the events that had shattered Cohen's life and propelled him down his dark path.

He focused on the Muslim Brotherhood operative, the one Cohen had been contracted to eliminate. The man's identity remained shrouded in secrecy. His name, a carefully constructed alias, led to dead ends and false trails. But the information he possessed, the access he held, was undeniable. The operative's infiltration attempt had been significant, potentially catastrophic. Why had someone been so desperate to silence him?

Pickens realized that his investigation was no longer a simple case of murder and robbery. It had evolved into something far more sinister, something that transcended national borders and touched upon the delicate balance of geopolitical power. The layers of deception were so meticulously crafted that each unraveling thread revealed a new labyrinth of secrets.

The phone rang, jarring him from his reverie. It was his superior, Captain Miller, his voice tight with urgency.

"Pickens, we have a problem. A big one. There's been another hit, similar M.O. to Cohen's victims, but this time...it's a high-ranking Israeli diplomat."

Pickens felt a chill crawl down his spine. The diplomat's murder was a blatant provocation, a message. It confirmed his suspicions—Cohen's network was not only alive, it was actively expanding its reach. The race was on again. Pickens knew he had to retrace Cohen's steps, to understand the intricate connections, the hidden alliances that had allowed him to operate with such impunity for so long. The city, once again, felt like a stage set for a deadly game, and he was once more thrust into the heart of it.

The ensuing weeks were a blur of interrogations, stakeouts, and dead ends. Pickens delved deeper into the murky world of international espionage and organized crime, encountering a cast of characters as morally ambiguous as Cohen himself.

He found himself navigating a treacherous landscape of double-crosses, betrayals, and shifting allegiances, the line between friend and foe constantly blurring. Each lead, each piece of evidence, seemed to point to a larger, more sinister conspiracy, a network far more extensive than he could have ever imagined. He started to see the patterns, the subtle connections that linked Cohen's actions to the ongoing geopolitical tensions in the Middle East and the simmering conflicts within the intelligence communities.

A contact in Mossad, someone who operated in the shadows, provided a cryptic piece of information: the gold reserves from the World Trade Center. It hadn't been a simple removal; it had been a calculated move, a secret deal struck in the shadows, a deal that linked high-ranking Israeli officials to powerful players in the world of organized crime.

The picture was starting to come into focus. Cohen hadn't simply been a rogue agent; he'd been a pawn in a much larger game, a game played by individuals who moved in the shadows, manipulating events from behind the scenes. The murders, the drug trafficking, the contract on the Muslim Brotherhood operative—all were orchestrated to serve their hidden agendas.

Pickens found himself in a perilous race against time, pursuing a network that stretched across continents and operated in the shadows. He realized that bringing down Cohen was just the first step in a larger, far more complex operation. He had to uncover the truth, no matter the cost. The hunt had only just begun, a grim ballet of deception and betrayal set against the backdrop of a city that held its breath, unaware of the storm brewing beneath its surface.

The lines between justice and vengeance, loyalty and betrayal, were more blurred than ever before. The weight of the world, it seemed, rested heavily on his shoulders. He was no longer just chasing a criminal; he was chasing a ghost, a phantom, a shadow of the past that threatened to engulf the present. The hunt continued, relentless and unforgiving, a chase that would define the rest of his life.

Miriams Testimony

The fluorescent lights of the interrogation room hummed, a monotonous counterpoint to the tremor in Miriam's voice. She sat across from Detective Tommy Pickens, her face pale and drawn, the vibrant energy he remembered from their brief, passionate affair extinguished, replaced by a haunted weariness. The coffee in her mug sat untouched, growing cold beside her trembling hands. Cohen's arrest had shaken her to her core, a seismic event that unearthed buried memories and long-suppressed truths. She knew she had to speak, to tell everything, even if it meant risking everything she held dear.

"It started... it started long before Sharon," she began, her voice barely a whisper, the words catching in her throat. "I was recruited by Mossad when I was still at university in Tel Aviv. They saw something in me... potential, they called it. I was good at languages, quick-witted, and had a knack for... persuasion." She paused, her eyes flitting nervously around the sterile room. "They groomed me, trained me, turned me into a weapon. It was thrilling at first—the sense of purpose, the danger, the secrecy."

Pickens leaned forward, his gaze intense. He'd known Miriam was a spy, a ghost in the shadows, but her words painted a far darker picture than he'd ever imagined. This wasn't about glamorous missions and heroic acts; this was a tale of manipulation, betrayal, and the slow erosion of a soul.

"My first assignment involved infiltrating a Palestinian activist group in the West Bank," she continued, her voice gaining strength. "It was brutal. I had to build trust, earn their confidence, and all the while, I was feeding information back to

Mossad. I saw things… things that still haunt me. The desperation, the anger, the sheer injustice of it all. It started to eat away at me—the moral compromises I had to make."

Miriam's testimony continued for hours. She detailed her operations, the people she had betrayed, the lives she had irrevocably touched. She spoke of the meticulous planning, the intricate webs of deceit, and the moments of sheer terror and calculated risk. She confessed to manipulating sources, exploiting vulnerabilities, and fabricating evidence to fit the narrative Mossad wanted. The work, she confessed, was a slow, agonizing process of moral degradation.

Pickens listened intently, meticulously taking notes. He was learning not only about Cohen but also about the underbelly of the Israeli intelligence apparatus, the shadowy operations, and the often-ruthless pragmatism that drove them. He learned of Cohen's early missions, his ruthlessness, and his ambition—an ambition that far outweighed his loyalty.

"Sharon… he was different," she said, her voice cracking. "He was ambitious, yes, but he also had a ruthless streak. I saw it firsthand. There were missions… where the orders were… unnecessary. Brutal. He enjoyed the power, the control." She looked down at her hands, as if trying to scrub away the memories. "He never hesitated to cross lines that even I found too far. He always claimed he was acting for the greater good, for the security of Israel, but I saw the truth. He was motivated by something darker, something more personal."

Miriam described the mission that had driven Cohen over the edge. It involved extracting vital information from a high-ranking Al-Qaeda operative who was planning a devastating attack on U.S. soil. Cohen had infiltrated the group, gained their trust, and managed to secure the intel, preventing a major terrorist attack. However, the Israeli government, she claimed, had secretly used his intel to accomplish their own agenda—the removal of gold reserves from the World Trade Center before the attack. Cohen had been given no credit, no recognition, only a cold dismissal. This act, she insisted, had broken him.

"He felt betrayed," Miriam explained, her voice laced with a hint of understanding. "He dedicated himself, risked everything, and for what? He was expendable. A tool to be used and discarded. That's when he started to unravel. The lines between right and wrong became blurred, and then... gone. He began working for the Israeli mob. He became someone else entirely."

Miriam described how Cohen's descent into the criminal underworld was both a consequence and a symptom of his deep-seated disillusionment. He started small, with petty crimes, then moved on to bigger operations. She recounted his drug deals, his betrayals, his acts of violence. Each story was a grim illustration of the seductive power of revenge and the corrupting influence of unchecked power.

She described Cohen's violent attack on her, the betrayal that left her physically and emotionally scarred. It wasn't a simple act of violence; it was a calculated act of cruelty, a testament to his descent into darkness. She described his growing paranoia, his increasing reliance on drugs and alcohol, and his insatiable thirst for vengeance.

"He always said he was fighting for justice," Miriam whispered, her eyes glistening with unshed tears. "But his version of justice was... different. He believed himself to be above the law, that his ends justified his means." The words hung heavy in the air, a chilling indictment of a man consumed by his own darkness.

Pickens pressed further, delving into the details of Cohen's later crimes. He learned of the contract to eliminate the Muslim Brotherhood infiltrator, the meticulously planned assassination attempt, and the complex web of contacts and associates involved. Miriam's testimony provided crucial details—names, dates, locations—pieces of a puzzle that Pickens had been painstakingly piecing together.

She described Cohen's targets—the wealthy Israelis he targeted for their perceived betrayal of the country, the Pakistani cab drivers who, to Cohen's twisted logic, represented a form of injustice. Each victim, she explained, had been chosen for a reason, a reason twisted and warped by Cohen's own fractured worldview.

The conversation stretched late into the night, a grim tableau of betrayal and despair. Miriam's testimony illuminated the dark undercurrents of international espionage, the moral ambiguities inherent in the world of intelligence, and the devastating consequences of unchecked power. As she spoke, Pickens realized that the Cohen case was far from over. It was a gateway, a key to understanding a much larger conspiracy. The more Miriam revealed, the more Pickens understood the vast network of corruption and violence that stretched across continents, a network that had not only tolerated Cohen's actions but perhaps even facilitated them.

The weight of the revelation settled on Pickens' shoulders. He had apprehended Cohen, but the battle was far from won. He was now on a collision course with forces far greater than he could have ever anticipated. The fight for justice was just beginning, a relentless pursuit that would push him to the brink. He looked at Miriam, her face etched with exhaustion and regret. He saw not just a witness, but a victim, a casualty of a war fought in the shadows, a war where the lines between right and wrong were irrevocably blurred. The road ahead was treacherous, filled with dangers both visible and unseen. But Pickens knew, with chilling certainty, that he couldn't stop. He had to uncover the truth, no matter the cost, even if it meant facing his own demons. The city outside the window, once a symbol of hope and opportunity, now seemed to reflect the darkness that lay at the heart of it all. The hunt continued.

A Race Against Time

The cold steel of the handcuffs bit into Cohen's wrists, a familiar sting that, oddly enough, soothed the adrenaline coursing through his veins. He had expected a struggle—a desperate fight against the inevitable—but the capture had been surprisingly... anticlimactic. The wiretap on Miriam's phone, a careless cigarette butt tossed in a world of meticulous planning, had been his undoing. He had underestimated her. He had underestimated the depth of her betrayal, and the chilling efficiency of the NYPD.

Now, sitting in the back of an unmarked police car, the city lights blurred into streaks of neon and shadow, Cohen felt an odd calm descend upon him. Years of deception, violence, and betrayal had culminated in this moment—a final, stark reckoning.

Pickens, however, felt anything but calm. Yes, he had caught Cohen, but the victory tasted like ash in his mouth. Miriam's testimony, though damning, had only scratched the surface. The threads of Cohen's intricate web of deceit led to shadowy figures, powerful players operating far beyond the reach of the NYPD. The contract to eliminate the Muslim Brotherhood operative—gleaned from intercepted communications—was a chilling confirmation of Cohen's descent into a world of international espionage and organized crime. The implications were staggering. This was no longer just a local crime spree; it was a geopolitical chess game, and Cohen was merely a pawn.

The urgency of the situation hit Pickens like a physical blow. Even in custody, Cohen remained a threat. His network, his connections, were still active, capable of wreaking havoc on a scale far greater than Pickens had ever imagined. The Muslim Brotherhood operative, whoever he was, remained at large, likely unaware of the danger he was in. He might possess sensitive information that could destabilize the already fragile balance of global power. Pickens needed to act. He needed to act fast.

The race against time had begun. He relayed the information to his superiors, the weight of his words pressing down on him like a physical burden. Initially skeptical, the higher-ups were soon persuaded by the evidence. The implications were too grave to ignore. What had begun as a seemingly straightforward investigation into a series of murders and robberies had now metastasized into a complex, multi-agency operation. The FBI, CIA, even Mossad were brought in, their resources converging on the same objective: neutralizing the remaining threats before more damage could be done.

The first step was identifying and apprehending the Muslim Brotherhood operative. Pickens and his team, working alongside federal agents and intelligence officers, plunged into the digital morass of Cohen's communications—tracing phone calls, emails, encrypted messages—a labyrinth of deceit and double-crosses. Each piece of information uncovered led to another layer of complexity, a deeper dive into the murky depths of international intrigue.

Days blurred into nights, fueled by caffeine and adrenaline. Pickens felt the familiar strain of pressure, the gnawing doubt that he might fail. The stakes were impossibly high. He knew that the lives of countless innocent people hung in the balance—not just in New York, but across the globe. The weight of responsibility threatened to crush him.

Then, the breakthrough came unexpectedly, in the form of a seemingly insignificant detail: a recurring code word used in Cohen's encrypted messages. An old Arabic proverb, obscure enough to evade detection by casual observers, yet significant enough to reveal the identity of the target. The operative was identified as Dr. Khalil Amin, a seemingly unassuming academic teaching political science at a prestigious university.

The next step was delicate, demanding precision and stealth. They couldn't afford a confrontation that would alert the operative and potentially trigger catastrophic consequences. They needed to apprehend him quietly, discreetly, before he could disappear or carry out his mission.

Surveillance was established on Dr. Amin's residence and workplace. The team watched and waited, meticulously monitoring his every move. The days and nights melted into a haze of anxiety and anticipation. The tension was palpable, the air thick with the silent pressure of imminent action.

The opportunity presented itself during a late-night meeting at a secluded café. Amin was meeting with a contact—a clandestine rendezvous that had the potential to destabilize the U.S. government if allowed to proceed. The raid was swift and precise. The agents moved like shadows, expertly neutralizing the contact before capturing Amin without incident.

Amin, upon arrest, offered little resistance. He was surprisingly calm—almost resigned to his fate. His interrogation, conducted by a team of seasoned intelligence professionals, revealed a chilling plot: Amin had been tasked with infiltrating the U.S. government, planting disinformation, and sowing discord. His mission was to create chaos—a wedge to exploit existing divisions and weaken American influence on the world stage.

The arrest of Amin was a significant victory, but the battle was far from over. The long shadow of Cohen's network still loomed, a web of deceit stretching far beyond their grasp. Pickens knew that Cohen's arrest had only been the beginning of a much larger investigation—a painstaking process of unraveling the intricate threads of a conspiracy that reached into the highest echelons of power.

The implications of Cohen's actions—his descent into a world of international crime and espionage—were staggering. He had been a pawn, a dangerous tool used by forces far beyond his understanding. Yet his actions had had devastating consequences. The lines between right and wrong had blurred, and Pickens found himself grappling with the moral ambiguities of his own pursuit of justice. He had caught Cohen, but the true reckoning was still to come. The network remained—its tentacles spreading across continents, its reach extending into the most powerful institutions. The hunt continued, a relentless pursuit that would test his limits, pushing him to the brink and forcing him to confront not only the darkness within the city but also the shadows within himself.

The city slept, unaware of the battles fought and won, and those yet to come. The game, however, was far from over. The shadows were deeper than Pickens had ever imagined. And the reckoning, it seemed, had only just begun.

Unraveling the Conspiracy

The interrogation room was stark, devoid of comfort. A single bare bulb hung from the ceiling, casting harsh shadows on the worn metal table where Cohen sat, his hands still numb from the cuffs. Pickens, his face etched with exhaustion, sat across from him, a thick file containing Cohen's history spread before him. The air was thick with unspoken accusations, the weight of years of deceit and violence pressing down on them both.

"You think you're clever, Cohen," Pickens finally said, his voice low and gravelly. "But you're just a pawn in a much larger game."

Cohen smirked, a flicker of defiance in his eyes. "And you think you're the one calling the shots?"

Pickens leaned forward, his gaze sharp and intense. "I'm starting to see the bigger picture. The Al-Qaeda bombing, the gold reserves… it wasn't some random act of terrorism. There were other players, other interests at stake. And you were right in the middle of it."

Cohen remained silent, letting the words hang in the air. He knew Pickens was right. He had been a pawn, a disposable asset in a high-stakes game of international intrigue. But the true extent of the conspiracy, the far-reaching network of power, was still a mystery.

The investigation deepened, revealing the intricacies of the Al-Qaeda plot. The meticulous planning, the seemingly impossible logistical coordination, suggested a level of sophistication far beyond the capabilities of a typical terrorist cell. Evidence emerged pointing to the bombing being more than an act of terror—it was a carefully orchestrated event with a specific financial and political objective. The removal of the Israeli gold reserves from the World Trade Center before the attack was no coincidence; it was a preemptive strike, executed with chilling precision.

Pickens began to see the scale of the operation. Initially, he had viewed Cohen as a ruthless criminal, a dangerous loose end. But now, Cohen was a key piece in a far more complex puzzle, one involving powerful figures both within and outside government circles. The trail led to shadowy figures within the Israeli intelligence community, individuals operating in the shadows, manipulating events for their own gain. Their goal wasn't just to destabilize the region, but to amass wealth and power through deception and manipulation.

The investigation uncovered a labyrinth of shell corporations, offshore accounts, and hidden investments in real estate and commodities, all linked to a clandestine network of individuals connected to organized crime and corrupt government officials. It became clear that the Al-Qaeda bombing was not an isolated incident but part of a broader financial conspiracy. The terrorist group had been manipulated—used as a pawn in a much larger game of financial power.

Pickens also uncovered a second layer to the conspiracy—a political one. The removal of the gold wasn't just about money; it served a political purpose. The act created a pretext for further intervention in the region, increasing global political influence and concentration of power. The subsequent war, spurred by the apparent terrorist attack, wasn't just a response to terror, but a consequence of the intricate web of deceit woven by powerful players manipulating the affair from behind the scenes.

As Pickens peeled back the layers of deception, he discovered that the conspiracy extended beyond Israel. He found evidence of collusion with powerful figures within the U.S. government, individuals who were not only aware of the plan but actively participated in its execution. Their complicity in allowing the operation to proceed without so much as raising an eyebrow raised serious questions about their loyalty and integrity.

Meanwhile, Miriam, still shaken from her ordeal, provided crucial information about Cohen's past, revealing details of his previous operations within Mossad. She confessed about their past assignments, their successes and failures, and the moral compromises they were forced to make. She described the pressure they faced from higher-ups, the disregard for human life, and the ethical implications of their actions. She painted a picture of a system within Mossad where the ends justified the means—even when those means were morally reprehensible.

As the pieces of the puzzle began to fall into place, Pickens understood the depth of the conspiracy. Cohen, despite his criminal activities, had been a victim of the system—a tool used by powerful forces for selfish motives. He had been a pawn, and those pulling the strings had skillfully avoided responsibility.

The investigation reached its climax with the arrest of several key figures involved in the conspiracy, including high-ranking government officials and individuals linked to international organized crime syndicates. The subsequent trial exposed the vast network of deceit and manipulation, revealing the deep corruption at the heart of the operation. The world watched in shock as the full extent of the conspiracy was unveiled, revealing the hidden agendas and dark dealings of those in power.

The case highlighted the fragility of trust and the corrupting allure of power. It underscored the lengths to which those with political ambition will go to achieve their goals. While Cohen's capture marked the end of his violent spree, the true reckoning extended far beyond his individual crimes. The wider investigation exposed a dark underbelly of international politics, with a network of shadowy figures manipulating events for their own gain. The consequences of their actions were far-reaching, destabilizing the region and causing widespread chaos. The trial revealed the depth of corruption that had festered for years, eroding trust in institutions and shaking the foundations of governments.

The final chapter of the story remained unwritten. The unmasking of the conspiracy, however, marked a turning point—a moment of reckoning for those in power. It sparked a wave of investigations, legal challenges, and political upheaval, forcing accountability on those who had used Cohen and others as pawns in their complex scheme. The unraveling of the conspiracy not only brought justice for Cohen's victims but also served as a stark reminder that in the world of international espionage, morality often blurs beyond recognition. The lines between right and wrong had become hopelessly intertwined, leaving an enduring question mark over the price of power and the cost of truth.

The city slept once more, but under a different sky—one darkened not by the shadow of a single man, but by the revelations of a conspiracy that had shaken the world. The game, however, remained far from over. The echoes of the reckoning resonated across continents.

Justice Served

The fluorescent lights of the interrogation room hummed, a low, constant buzz that seemed to mirror the frantic pulse of Cohen's heart. He had expected defiance—a final, fierce stand against the system that had chewed him up and spat him out. But instead, an unexpected calm had settled over him, a weary resignation to the inevitable. Pickens, however, radiated no such serenity. The exhaustion etched into his features had deepened, now replaced by a grim, unyielding determination. The file lay discarded on the table, its contents—a damning record of Cohen's life of crime—now irrelevant, overshadowed by the sheer weight of his confession.

Cohen had spoken—not out of remorse, not from a sudden surge of conscience, but driven by a chilling pragmatism. He had laid bare the conspiracy, unraveling the intricate web of deceit that stretched from the murky depths of the Moroccan underworld to the polished halls of the Israeli government. He named names, detailed transactions, painted a picture so vivid and damning that even the most seasoned lawyers would struggle to untangle it. He spoke of the gold, the Al-Qaeda plot, and the brutal betrayal of Miriam—each detail recounted with chilling precision, each lie methodically deconstructed.

It was a confession born not of regret but of cold calculation. Cohen had realized that silence would be his death sentence; cooperation, grudging though it was, offered him a sliver of hope—an opportunity to manipulate the narrative, to perhaps even gain some measure of control over his fate, however slim that chance might be.

The confession reverberated through the establishment like an earthquake. The Israeli government, already reeling from the initial scandal, teetered on the brink of collapse. Investigations, once whispers in shadowy backrooms, now roared to life, pulling powerful figures into the harsh, unforgiving light of public scrutiny. The once-muted whispers of corruption had grown into thundering accusations, as officials scrambled to protect themselves, their careers, their reputations, and, most urgently, their freedom. News outlets around the world consumed the story, headlines screaming of betrayal, deception, and the devastating cost of unchecked power. Initially skeptical, the public slowly began to grasp the full scale of the conspiracy—the breathtaking audacity of a plot to manipulate a global event for national gain.

Meanwhile, Pickens watched from the sidelines, a detached observer caught in the maelstrom. He had pursued Cohen with relentless fervor, driven by a combination of professional obligation and personal vendetta. Now, the chase was over, the prey captured, but the victory felt hollow, tainted by the disturbing truths that had been uncovered. Cohen's confession had inadvertently dragged Pickens into a world far larger and more dangerous than he had ever imagined. The investigation, far from concluding, had morphed into a sprawling legal battle—a confrontation with entrenched power and formidable adversaries.

Miriam, shaken but resolute, emerged from the shadows, her testimony now a vital piece in the puzzle. Once collateral damage in Cohen's ruthless game of power and wealth, she was no longer a mere pawn. Her testimony was not born of vengeance but of an unyielding need for truth—a desire to see justice prevail, not just for herself but for all those who had fallen victim to Cohen's machinations. She spoke of Cohen's descent into darkness, the chilling transformation from a loyal agent into a remorseless criminal—a metamorphosis driven by disillusionment and a thirst for revenge against a system he believed had wronged him. Her words gave a human face to the cold, calculated actions of a man she once loved and trusted.

The trial itself became a spectacle. The courtroom, packed with reporters and spectators, buzzed with anticipation. Cohen, his demeanor a chilling blend of indifference and controlled rage, sat impassively as accusations flew. The prosecution presented a mountain of evidence, painting a vivid picture of Cohen's criminal enterprise. His defense, however, was a calculated maneuver, attempting to recast him as a victim—a pawn manipulated by a corrupt system. They argued that his actions, while undeniably criminal, were the direct result of his betrayal by Mossad, a consequence of the government's ruthless disregard for the lives of its agents.

The strategy was bold, a gamble designed to deflect blame and shift responsibility to those in power.

The jury, burdened by the weight of the evidence, deliberated for days. The trial had exposed a cesspool of corruption—a network of deceit that reached the highest echelons of power. The verdict, when it came, was a resounding condemnation of Cohen's actions, but also an implicit acknowledgment of the systemic failures that had allowed him to operate with impunity for so long. He was convicted on multiple counts of murder, conspiracy, and various other crimes, sentenced to life without parole. Yet the victory felt incomplete, a hollow echo in the vast landscape of justice.

Cohen's downfall, rather than bringing closure, ignited a political firestorm. The conspiracy he had exposed triggered a cascade of investigations, leading to the arrests and indictments of numerous government officials, both Israeli and American. The revelations rocked the foundations of international trust, exposing the fragility of alliances and the ease with which national interests could be manipulated by those in power. The echoes of the scandal reverberated across continents, causing a reassessment of national security protocols and sparking a profound reevaluation of the morality behind international espionage.

In the end, Cohen's capture stood as a stark reminder of the human cost of ambition, the destructive potential of unchecked power, and the insidious nature of corruption. Justice, it seemed, had been served—but not in the way anyone had expected. The price of truth was steep, paid in blood and betrayal, leaving a legacy of suspicion, mistrust, and lingering questions about the true nature of power and its limits. The city, once again, slept, but the shadows of the conspiracy continued to loom, a chilling reminder of the lengths some will go to in the pursuit of power—and the devastating consequences of unchecked ambition. The game was over, but the echoes of the reckoning would resonate for generations to come. The world, forever altered by the revelations, would now have to grapple with the moral ambiguity of Cohen's actions and the systemic failures that had allowed his descent into darkness. The question lingered: Had justice truly been served, or had the pursuit of justice only exposed a deeper, more insidious rot at the heart of the global system? The answer, like the city's slumber, remained elusive—a quiet whisper on the wind.

Early Life

The scent of eucalyptus and chlorine lingered in my memory, a phantom odor from a life spent in the perpetual grip of near-drowning. The training pool at the Mossad facility outside Tel Aviv – cold, unyielding, a baptism of brutal reality. It was here, submerged in the biting chill, that I first grasped the true nature of loyalty, the crushing weight of secrets, and the seductive allure of betrayal. My father, a respected judge with unwavering faith in justice, would have been horrified. He had always championed the integrity of the law, a stark contrast to the shadowy world I was about to enter.

I was barely twenty, a fresh-faced recruit brimming with a fierce desire to serve. My family, steeped in Zionist ideals, had instilled in me a profound sense of patriotism. I saw myself as a modern-day David, fighting for Israel's survival against a Goliath of enemies. This naïve idealism was quickly tempered by the harsh realities of training. We were pushed to our physical and mental limits. Sleep deprivation became a constant companion, the looming threat of failure a gnawing anxiety. The instructors, battle-hardened veterans of countless covert operations, were masters of psychological manipulation, stripping away our vulnerabilities, leaving only the raw, ruthless efficiency that Mossad demanded.

The curriculum was not merely physical. We studied languages, cryptography, explosives, hand-to-hand combat, and the delicate art of deception. We learned to disappear, to become ghosts, to blend into any environment. We learned to lie convincingly, without hesitation. This was the craft of espionage – a twisted morality where the ends always justified the means, no matter the cost.

My early missions were small, insignificant cogs in the vast machine of intelligence gathering. Surveillance, data collection, the meticulous assembly of seemingly unrelated fragments of information. Each success, no matter how minor, fed the growing confidence and arrogance that would eventually lead to my undoing. I reveled in the thrill of the chase, the intellectual puzzle of unearthing secrets, the intoxicating power of controlling information.

One mission stands out. A seemingly innocuous meeting in a bustling Marrakech souk, orchestrated to gather intelligence on a suspected arms dealer. The air was thick with the scent of spices, incense, and sweat. The cacophony of haggling merchants, braying donkeys, and the mournful call to prayer created a dizzying assault on the senses. Yet I moved through it all with unsettling calm, a ghost observing from the shadows. I was a chameleon, adapting, observing, learning.

The target, a portly man with shifty eyes and a nervous laugh, met with a shadowy figure, their face mostly concealed by a djellaba. Their exchange, hushed and furtive, was conducted entirely in Darija, a dialect I had mastered during my training. I shadowed them for hours, meticulously recording their movements, noting their meeting points, and interpreting their hand signals – a silent language only they understood.

The operation was a success. I gathered enough intelligence to identify the arms dealer's network, a crucial victory in the ongoing battle against terrorism. Yet, even then, a nagging unease began to creep in. The casually cruel efficiency of the organization, the way individual lives were sacrificed for national security, began to sow seeds of doubt. It wasn't just the enemy we were fighting; it was ourselves, our own internal demons.

The years that followed were a blur of clandestine operations, dangerous assignments, and moral compromises. I became a ghost, flitting through the darkest corners of the world. I witnessed unspeakable cruelty, participated in covert operations that blurred the lines between right and wrong. I learned to compartmentalize my emotions, suppressing the guilt, the regret, the ever-growing sense of alienation. My life became a fragmented series of memories, snapshots of violence and betrayal. Each mission left a deeper scar, a mark carved into the very fabric of my soul.

The constant pressure, the ever-present threat of exposure, took its toll. The masks I wore began to slip, revealing cracks in my carefully constructed persona. Sleep became a battlefield, haunted by the faces of those I had betrayed or, worse, killed.

The dissonance between my idealized image of myself as a champion of justice and the grim reality of my actions grew. I had traded my father's unwavering belief in the rule of law for the shadowy world of espionage, where morality was a luxury I could no longer afford. My early idealism eroded, replaced by a cynical pragmatism. I became a ghost, haunting my own past. The ghost of Marrakech, where I first witnessed the true face of my chosen profession, became a haunting reminder of the price I had already paid and would continue to pay for my life as a Mossad agent.

One night, amidst the chaos of a brutal operation in Beirut, I looked at my reflection in a shattered mirror. The image staring back at me wasn't the idealistic young man who had eagerly joined Mossad. It was a stranger, his eyes cold and hard, a face etched with the weariness of a thousand sleepless nights, stained with the blood of unseen enemies. It was the first time I truly saw the transformation – the metamorphosis from a naïve recruit to a cynical operator, a ghost moving through the shadows.

I began to question my loyalty, my motivations, the very foundations of my existence within the organization. The line between right and wrong had become utterly blurred. I was constantly juggling different identities, each a carefully constructed facade designed to deceive and manipulate.

The psychological strain was immense. The constant fear, the weight of secrets, the moral compromises – they were slowly suffocating me, eroding my soul. The once-bright flame of idealism had dimmed, replaced by a cold, calculating pragmatism. The betrayals, both by my superiors and by those I had worked with, left me deeply disillusioned. The price of loyalty was too high, and I began to question whether it was even worth paying.

My relationships were shallow, marred by suspicion and deceit. Intimacy became a dangerous game, a potential vulnerability that could be exploited by both my enemies and allies. Even Miriam, my girlfriend at the time, was part of this complicated dance of secrecy and betrayal. She knew what I did for a living, but the true extent of my actions, my moral compromises, remained hidden – a dark secret I could not share.

The ghost of Marrakech, the phantom scent of eucalyptus and chlorine, the chilling memory of betrayal – these are all part of the price I paid for my time in Mossad. A price I still pay today, years after leaving that life behind. The world has changed, but the ghost remains, a constant reminder of the choices I've made and the life I could have led. The life my father always dreamed of for me – one of justice, fairness, and integrity – a life far removed from the shadows where I now reside.

The Seeds of Disillusionment

The shimmering mirage of the Negev Desert danced before me, the relentless sun pounding down on my neck like a blacksmith's hammer. It blurred the already hazy line between reality and the carefully constructed illusion I'd become. My mission, codenamed "Desert Bloom," seemed straightforward on paper: infiltrate a suspected Al-Qaeda cell operating out of a remote Bedouin village. In truth, it was a viper's nest of deceit, suspicion, and brutal pragmatism.

I was young then—barely out of training, brimming with the naïve idealism the Mossad had so expertly cultivated. I believed in the righteousness of our cause, in the unwavering moral compass that guided our actions. That belief, like the delicate desert flowers, was about to wither and die.

My handler, Avram, a man whose eyes gleamed with the cold, calculating sharpness of polished obsidian, had briefed me thoroughly. The cell was planning a major attack, the target unknown. My task was to gain their trust, to become one of them, and feed information back to headquarters. Avram emphasized the importance of discretion—of remaining unseen, unheard. He spoke of the sacrifices required, the compromises that needed to be made in the name of national security. At the time, these words sounded like heroic proclamations, the solemn utterances of a seasoned warrior preparing his novice for battle. The reality, however, was far more insidious.

The weeks I spent embedded with the cell became a blur of harsh landscapes, whispered conversations, and the ever-present threat of discovery. I learned their language, their customs, their deeply ingrained hatred of Israel. I shared their meals, their prayers, their anxieties. I saw their humanity, their capacity for love and loyalty—qualities that shattered the carefully constructed image the Mossad had painted for me. These weren't mindless fanatics; they were men driven by desperation, by a history of injustice and oppression. Their anger, though misdirected, felt almost justified.

It was during this time that I first encountered Omar, the cell's enigmatic leader. He was a man of contradictions: ruthless and calculating yet possessed of a surprising intellectual curiosity. We spent hours discussing politics, philosophy, even poetry. He spoke of a just world, of self-determination, of a future free from the shackles of foreign intervention. His words resonated deeply with me, stirring a sense of unease that went beyond my assignment. They chipped away at the carefully constructed foundation of my loyalty, revealing cracks of doubt I had never allowed myself to acknowledge.

The turning point came unexpectedly. The cell's planned attack was far larger and more ambitious than we had anticipated. It wasn't just a bombing; it was a coordinated assault designed to cripple Israel's infrastructure. The intelligence I gathered allowed the Mossad to disrupt the plot, but the method was… unsettling.

The day before the planned attack, our intelligence revealed that Israel was moving its gold reserves out of the World Trade Center in New York. A meticulously planned operation, coordinated with American authorities, who remained oblivious to the true reason for the transfer. Our actions, seemingly a preemptive strike, were in reality a cover for this massive financial maneuver. The timing was impeccable; it made the entire operation appear to be a fortunate coincidence to the outside world. Yet, I couldn't shake the sense of unease—the feeling that we were playing a game far more dangerous than we had ever been told. This felt less like precise strategic maneuvering and more like organized chaos, like being caught in a current too strong to fight against, or a storm destined to wreak havoc.

The attack was thwarted, and I was hailed as a hero. Avram shook my hand, his usual cold exterior softened by a rare display of emotion. He praised my bravery, my dedication, my resourcefulness. But his words felt hollow, devoid of genuine appreciation. They sounded more like an acknowledgment of a debt paid, a job well done, rather than recognition of a truly significant achievement. My reward was a pat on the back, a quick promotion, and a transfer to a desk job in a stuffy Tel Aviv office—far removed from the adrenaline-fueled world of espionage. The cold detachment of it all made me feel isolated, adrift.

The accolades felt empty, the praise meaningless. The moral complexities of the operation, the chilling pragmatism of the higher-ups, left a deep scar on my soul. I saw the government, the institution I had sworn to serve, not as a beacon of justice, but as a ruthless player in a high-stakes game where morality was merely a pawn, sacrificed at the whim of expediency. The idealism that had fueled my early years crumbled to dust, leaving behind only disillusionment and a profound sense of betrayal. The ghosts of the Negev Desert whispered tales of deception and betrayal, forever etching the seeds of my disillusionment onto my heart. The scent of eucalyptus and chlorine, the cold water of the training pool, now held only the bitter taste of betrayal.

My frustration festered. I felt like a pawn in a game orchestrated by forces far beyond my comprehension. The knowledge of the covert gold transfer gnawed at my conscience—a constant reminder of the ethical compromises the Mossad was willing to make. The lies, the deception, the casual disregard for human life—all of it began to unravel the carefully constructed image of the Mossad as a force for good. I could no longer reconcile my actions with my conscience. The very foundation of my loyalty was crumbling.

My requests for further missions were met with cold indifference. The adrenaline rush of clandestine operations was replaced by the soul-crushing monotony of paperwork and endless meetings. The cold, sterile environment of the office felt like a prison—a stark contrast to the dangerous, exhilarating world I had known. The feeling of betrayal festered, transforming into a deep-seated resentment, which fueled my descent into the criminal underworld. It was a slow descent, beginning with small compromises, minor betrayals, which quickly spiraled into a full-on moral corruption.

The world I had known, the world I had so fervently defended, had revealed itself to be far more complicated, far more corrupt, than I could have ever imagined. The line between right and wrong had blurred into an indistinguishable gray, leaving me adrift in a sea of moral ambiguity. The seeds of disillusionment had taken root, and they were growing fast, strangling any remaining vestiges of my former loyalty. The path ahead, I knew, would be treacherous.

My descent into darkness was gradual, almost imperceptible at first. It began with small acts of defiance—subtle ways of undermining the authority that had so cruelly abandoned me. I found myself drawn to the shadows, to the murky world of deceit and subterfuge. The rules, the codes of conduct, the very principles I had once sworn to uphold, now seemed irrelevant, insignificant. They no longer offered any solace or sense of purpose. The idealism that had once burned so brightly in my soul was now a smoldering ember, threatened with extinction.

The allure of power—the intoxicating sense of control, the ability to manipulate events and people—became increasingly appealing. It was a way to reclaim the agency that had been so ruthlessly stolen from me. The world of espionage, with its intricate webs of deceit and clandestine operations, had prepared me well for this life. I possessed the skills, the knowledge, the ruthless efficiency required to thrive in this new world. I was a wolf in sheep's clothing, a chameleon capable of blending seamlessly into any environment. The world had wronged me, and now it would pay. The seeds of disillusionment had yielded a bitter, intoxicating fruit. The taste of betrayal was finally mine to savor.

The transition wasn't easy, but it was complete. The memories of the training pool, the desert sun, the cold hand of Avram— they were now distant echoes, reminders of a life I had left behind. The new life, though dangerous, offered a certain perverse satisfaction. It was a life ruled by instinct and immediate gratification, devoid of the ethical quandaries that had plagued me for so long. In the chaotic world of organized crime, there was no room for idealism, no place for sentimentality. There was only survival. And I was determined to survive. I would thrive, even if it meant sullying my hands with blood. The price of disillusionment was high, but I was ready to pay it.

The Making of a Spy

The desert wind lashed sand against my face, a gritty reminder of the brutal truths I had chosen to face. Marrakech—a city of vivid contrasts, where opulent palaces stood in sharp opposition to crumbling medinas—became my new crucible. My Mossad training had been rigorous, a relentless process designed to forge agents capable of withstanding unimaginable pressure. We were taught to vanish, to blend effortlessly into any environment, to extract information from even the most unwilling sources. We were schooled in the art of deception, the subtle nuances of manipulation, and the chilling efficiency of violence. But it was in Marrakech, in the heart of its labyrinthine souks and shadowed alleyways, that I truly learned the price of survival.

The transition from idealistic operative to hardened criminal wasn't a sudden metamorphosis but a slow erosion of morality—a gradual and agonizing death of the soul. It began with small compromises, minor transgressions rationalized as necessary evils: a silenced informant, a hastily altered report, a carefully placed bribe. Each act was a small crack in the foundation of my integrity, widening with each passing day until the entire structure collapsed. My instructors had warned us about the moral compromises inherent in the profession, the constant juggling act between right and wrong. Yet, no classroom lecture could prepare me for the chilling reality. Theoretical exercises were nothing compared to the weight of a life hanging in the balance, the cold certainty of death ever-present by my side.

My instructors, men and women hardened by years of clandestine operations, were masters of psychological warfare. They knew how to break you down, to strip away your vulnerabilities, and to exploit your deepest fears. They pushed us to our limits, both physically and mentally, forcing us to confront our own mortality. The training was a ceaseless test of endurance—a grueling marathon of physical conditioning, weapons training, and interrogation techniques. We learned to fight hand-to-hand, to wield a knife with lethal precision, to disarm an opponent in the blink of an eye. We underwent intense psychological evaluations designed to assess our resilience, our ability to withstand torture, and our capacity for deception. They wanted to break us, to mold us into something more efficient. And, in a way, they succeeded.

The ethical dilemmas weren't explicitly taught but subtly instilled through the actions and decisions we were forced to make during training exercises. The simulated scenarios pushed us into morally gray areas, forcing us to make impossible choices with life-altering consequences. We were taught that sometimes, the ends justify the means—a philosophy that would later come back to haunt me. The line between right and wrong blurred, becoming a shifting, unreliable entity. What had begun as a clear-cut mission to protect Israel's interests slowly morphed into a relentless pursuit of self-preservation, fueled by a burning resentment toward the very system I had once served.

My disillusionment crept in slowly—a creeping doubt, a persistent question mark over every action. The initial pride and patriotism, the sense of purpose that had once fueled my dedication, gradually gave way to cold, hard cynicism. I began to see the cracks in the carefully constructed façade of the Mossad—the compromises, the double-dealing, the blatant disregard for human life. The official narrative, the righteous justifications, began to ring hollow, replaced by a chilling realization: I was a pawn in a larger game, a disposable asset in a brutal, unforgiving world.

The final straw came with the Al-Qaeda bombing plot. I had infiltrated the terrorist cell, gathered crucial intelligence—information that had allowed the Israeli government to preemptively remove their gold reserves from the World Trade Center. I had averted a potential catastrophe, but my contribution was ignored, unacknowledged. My reward was a mere pat on the back and a swift transfer to a dead-end assignment. The betrayal cut deep, a wound that festered and festered. It was in that moment, sitting in the arid dust of the Negev, watching the sun set on my shattered idealism, that I made the decision to walk away.

But walking away wasn't as simple as I had imagined. The Mossad didn't easily let go of its assets. My connections, my skills, my knowledge—they were too valuable to discard. The transition to the underworld was jarring, a brutal baptism into a world without rules and without mercy. Marrakech, with its maze-like souks and shadowy figures, was the perfect place to disappear, to reinvent myself. The organized crime network in Marrakech was a complex web of rivalries, alliances, deceit, and betrayal. I started small, using my skills to navigate the treacherous currents of the underworld. My past experiences were assets in this new life, but I was no longer operating for Israel, no longer bound by their ideology. I had found a new purpose, a new loyalty— to myself.

The life I built in Marrakech was a far cry from the structured world of the Mossad. It was a world of instant gratification and fleeting alliances, a world where loyalty was a commodity traded for money and power. The moral compass that had once guided my actions was now discarded, a relic of a bygone era. My days were filled with a dangerous cocktail of clandestine meetings, high-stakes deals, and violent confrontations. I learned the language of the streets—the unspoken rules of survival. The skills I had honed in the Mossad proved invaluable, allowing me to manipulate and outmaneuver my opponents. But this wasn't about espionage; it was about power, control, survival.

The adrenaline rush was addictive, a potent drug that masked the gnawing emptiness within. I moved through the city like a ghost—unseen, unheard, yet always present. The luxury hotels, lavish casinos, opulent villas—these became my playgrounds, places where I could play the charming outsider, the successful businessman, the man who had everything. But the mask slipped, revealing the darkness beneath. The violent assault on Miriam, my former lover and fellow spy, was the breaking point—the moment I truly lost myself.

My ruthless efficiency, honed through Mossad training, made me a valuable asset in the underworld, but it also made me a dangerous enemy. The betrayal and violence I inflicted, the lives I irrevocably altered, were a stark testament to the transformation I had undergone. The price of my disillusionment was steep, and I paid it in full, one brutal act at a time. The ghost of Marrakech— that was me. A specter haunting the city's shadowy corners, a reminder that even the most carefully constructed illusions can crumble under the weight of betrayal and self-destruction. And the city, with its labyrinthine alleys and suffocating heat, seemed to embrace my darkness, nurturing my descent into the abyss. The game was far from over. The past, like a relentless shadow, was beginning to catch up.

First Missions

The air hung thick and heavy with the scent of jasmine and decay. My first mission for Mossad wasn't glamorous—far from it. It involved a low-level Hezbollah operative, a petty thief named Khalil who dealt in stolen antiquities. He wasn't a major player, but he was a link, a thread in a much larger tapestry of illicit activity. My orders were simple: extract information, neutralize the threat. Neutralize. The word lingered in the air, a chilling echo of the violence to come.

I found Khalil in a dimly lit Casablanca bar, the air thick with cigarette smoke and the murmur of hushed conversations. He was nursing a glass of amber liquid, his eyes darting nervously around the room. Younger than I had expected—barely out of his teens—his face was etched with a weariness that belied his age. I approached him, a casual observer, a stranger lost in the labyrinthine world of the bar. We talked, I listened, probing gently at first, then pressing harder as I gained his confidence. He was easy to manipulate, desperate for acceptance and affirmation. He spilled his secrets like cheap wine.

The information he gave me was insignificant in the grand scheme of things, but it was a start. It led to another contact, a smuggler operating out of Tangier named Omar, a man who dealt in weapons and explosives. Omar was a tougher nut to crack, a hardened criminal with a network of informants and enforcers. I needed to play a different game with him—one of intimidation and implied violence. Mossad had trained me well in the art of psychological warfare. I used the information I'd gleaned from Khalil to leverage my way into Omar's confidence, subtly suggesting my own connections to powerful figures. He underestimated me, mistaking my quiet demeanor for weakness.

Omar's operation was surprisingly sophisticated—an efficient machine moving weapons and explosives across borders with alarming precision. His network stretched across North Africa, reaching deep into the heart of the Sahara Desert. My mission was to gather intelligence, map his network, and identify his key contacts and suppliers. It was meticulous work, requiring patience and precision. I spent weeks shadowing Omar, observing his routines, identifying his patterns. I learned to anticipate his movements, to predict his reactions. I became a ghost, a silent observer, blending seamlessly into the bustling streets of Tangier.

During one of my stakeouts, I witnessed something that changed the trajectory of my mission. Omar was meeting with a high-ranking member of the Algerian military, a man who was supplying him with weapons-grade explosives. This was far beyond a simple smuggling operation; it was a conspiracy of international proportions. I knew instantly that this information was too big for me to handle alone. I needed to report it to my superiors in Tel Aviv. But doing so meant acknowledging the scope of the conspiracy, the potential threat it posed. And that meant accepting the inevitable escalation. The risks involved were far greater than initially anticipated.

The report I filed was terse, factual, and devoid of emotion. But it sparked a chain of events that would forever alter my perception of Mossad—and my own role within it. The operation was escalated. A special team was assembled, and a covert mission was launched. I was integrated into the team as an observer, a silent witness. I watched as seasoned operatives moved into position, their expertise and professionalism a stark contrast to my own unorthodox methods. Their dedication to the mission was unwavering; their loyalty unquestionable.

But even as I observed, a cold realization began to set in. The methods employed by the team were ruthless, efficient, and bordering on amoral. They weren't just collecting intelligence; they were eliminating threats. They weren't merely disrupting terrorist networks; they were dismantling lives. I saw the disregard for human life, the casual cruelty that was often necessary to achieve the mission's objectives.

It was a brutal lesson in the realities of espionage—a stark contrast to the idealized image I had once held.

The operation culminated in a series of raids and arrests. The Algerian military officer was captured, along with several key members of Omar's smuggling ring. The operation was deemed a success, but the cost was high. Lives were lost—not just on the enemy side, but on ours as well. Collateral damage. The term felt hollow, inadequate to describe the devastation it caused. The mission was a success, measured in intelligence gathered and threats neutralized. But the human cost was becoming increasingly unacceptable to me.

My disillusionment began subtly, with a growing unease, a sense of disquiet festering beneath the surface of my professional facade. I questioned the ethics of the mission, the methods employed, and the consequences of our actions. Was this what I wanted? Was this what I had dedicated my life to?

The next mission was different. It was personal. A low-level informant, a man I had once helped, needed assistance. He had become embroiled in a deadly dispute with a rival faction within the Palestinian Liberation Organization—a dispute that had escalated into a brutal power struggle. Initially reluctant to get involved, something about this mission resonated differently. This wasn't about national security or geopolitical strategy. This was about loyalty—an unspoken bond formed in the shadows.

I made the decision to assist my informant, despite the obvious risks. My loyalty to Mossad was fraying at the edges, replaced by a sense of moral ambiguity—the belief that some battles should be fought outside the official frameworks. I helped him escape, using skills honed over years of operating in the shadows. But helping him meant violating protocol, breaking established rules. It was a dangerous game to play.

The consequences of my actions were swift and severe. I was reprimanded, censured, my future with Mossad hanging precariously in the balance. But I didn't regret my decision. I had made a choice—a conscious decision to prioritize loyalty over institutional obedience. And for the first time, I felt a sense of liberation—a freedom from the constraints of the organization. The seeds of my rebellion had been sown. The ghost of Marrakech was beginning to take shape.

The Cost of Loyalty

The Marrakech sun beat down on me, merciless and unforgiving. It was a different kind of heat than the sterile, controlled environments of Mossad's training facilities. This was raw, visceral heat that seeped into your bones, mirroring the simmering anger that had taken root within me. The thrill of the chase, the calculated risk, the adrenaline rush – all of it had faded, replaced by a gnawing emptiness. The liberation I'd once felt after defying Mossad was quickly slipping away, replaced by a profound loneliness. My actions had consequences, far-reaching and devastating.

I'd traded the structured world of espionage for the chaotic, unpredictable life of a criminal. The rules were different now – more brutal, less forgiving. Loyalty, once a sacred oath, had twisted into a game of survival. In Mossad, betrayal was a capital offense. Here, in the labyrinthine alleys of Marrakech, it was currency.

The faces of my victims swam before my eyes – Khalil, the petty thief; the nameless men I'd eliminated in the name of national security or personal gain. Their faces, blurred and distorted by the haze of memory and regret, haunted my dreams, their silent screams echoing in the suffocating heat. I had justified my actions then, telling myself I was serving a greater purpose, a higher calling. But the lies felt hollow now, their justifications crumbling beneath the weight of my guilt.

Miriam. Her face, once vibrant and full of life, was etched in my mind, a constant reminder of my betrayal. The violence, the brutality – it was a stain on my soul that no amount of Moroccan sunshine could ever wash away. The love we once shared had shattered, replaced by a chasm of hatred and resentment. I had convinced myself she was expendable, a pawn in a larger game, but the truth was far more insidious. I had chosen self-preservation over love, loyalty over compassion. The cost was far higher than I had ever imagined.

The money, the lavish lifestyle, the power – they all felt meaningless now. The fleeting pleasures were overshadowed by a constant sense of dread, a looming fear of discovery. I was living on borrowed time, a fugitive running from both the law and my own conscience. Sleep became a luxury, replaced by fits of paranoia, punctuated by nightmares that replayed my past transgressions in vivid, horrifying detail.

My former colleagues in Mossad, the men and women I had once considered family, were now potential enemies. My loyalty to them, once absolute, had evaporated. I was an outcast, a pariah, a ghost moving through a world that no longer recognized me. The camaraderie, the shared sense of purpose, the brotherhood of arms – it was all gone, replaced by chilling isolation.

The Israeli mob, the ruthless criminals I had aligned myself with, offered no solace. They were predators, driven by greed and ambition, devoid of any real loyalty or compassion. They were willing to use me, exploit me, then discard me the moment I became expendable. I had become one of them – a reflection of their darkness, a testament to my own moral decay.

The constant threat of exposure was suffocating. The shadow of Mossad loomed over me, their reach extending far beyond the borders of Israel. I knew they were looking for me, hunting me, and their patience was waning. Every shadow, every unfamiliar face, felt like a potential threat, a sign that my past was finally catching up with me.

My work with the Muslim Brotherhood contract only exacerbated my sense of isolation and despair. Eliminating a potential threat to the US government felt more like an act of self-preservation than patriotism. The lines had blurred; my moral compass had spun wildly out of control. I was operating in a gray zone where right and wrong were subjective, and survival was the only constant.

The irony wasn't lost on me. I had once sworn to protect my country, to fight for justice. Now I was engaged in acts of violence, motivated by personal gain and fear. The transformation was complete. I was a ghost, a shadow of my former self, adrift in a sea of deceit and betrayal.

Even the fleeting moments of satisfaction, the adrenaline rush of successfully completing a contract, were quickly replaced by a deep sense of emptiness. The thrill had vanished, replaced by a gnawing hollowness that mirrored the decay I saw all around me in Marrakech. The city, a vibrant tapestry of cultures and contradictions, felt as lost and fragmented as I was.

I found myself spending hours staring at the vast expanse of the Sahara Desert, its endless dunes mirroring the vast emptiness within me. I wondered if there was a way back, a path to redemption, but the answer remained elusive – a mirage in the shimmering heat. The cost of loyalty, I realized, was far greater than I had ever imagined. It was a price paid not only in blood and violence, but in the loss of my soul.

The relentless pursuit by Detective Pickens added another layer to my torment. His investigation, initially unrelated to my activities, was slowly drawing closer – a tightening noose around my neck. His relationship with Miriam, the woman I had betrayed, added a personal stake to his pursuit. He was more than just a police detective; he was a vengeful angel, seeking justice for the pain I had inflicted.

The weight of my past actions bore down on me. The memories, once suppressed, clawed their way to the surface, bringing with them a torrent of guilt and self-loathing. I was trapped, caught in a web of my own making, with no escape in sight. My once-sharp mind, honed by years of training and experience, now felt clouded by paranoia and self-doubt.

The familiar scent of jasmine, once a symbol of beauty and serenity, now felt like a bitter reminder of my past life – the life I had abandoned, and the life I could never reclaim. The ghosts of Marrakech were not just the specters of my past, but the embodiment of my fractured identity. I was a broken man, a shell of my former self, haunted by the consequences of my choices. The cost of loyalty, I realized, was not measured in dollars or lives, but in the immeasurable loss of one's humanity. The price was steep, and it was a price I was paying every single day.

The end, however, was not yet in sight. The game, it seemed, was far from over. The shadows still danced in the corners of my mind, whispering of betrayals yet to come.

Miriams Past

The flickering gaslight cast long, jagged shadows across Miriam's face, accentuating the faint lines etched around her eyes—lines that told a story not just of age, but of a life lived perilously close to the edge. She sat opposite me, the half-empty glass of amber liquid swirling in her hand, the ice clinking a stark counterpoint to the rhythmic thump-thump-thump of the ancient Marrakech city beyond the thick, hand-carved door. The air was thick with the scent of spices and secrets—a fitting ambiance for the story she was about to unravel.

It was a story she had never willingly shared, not with anyone. But the events of the past few weeks—Sharon's capture, the near-death experience—had shattered the walls she'd so carefully constructed around her past. The truth, as she confessed, was as murky and treacherous as the Casablanca souk.

She had been born into privilege, the daughter of a prominent Israeli diplomat stationed in London. Her childhood was a tapestry woven with threads of gilded luxury and clandestine meetings. She learned early on that appearances were deceiving, that the polished veneer of diplomatic life often concealed a dark underbelly of intrigue and betrayal. Her father, a man of impeccable reputation in public, was privately entrenched in operations far removed from the world of formal diplomacy.

At a young age, he introduced her to the world of espionage— not as a formal recruit, but as a vital, albeit unwitting, asset. She learned to observe, to listen, to interpret the subtle nuances of human interaction. She mastered the art of reading body language, deciphering coded messages, and blending seamlessly into any environment. It was a brutal education, one that stripped away her innocence and replaced it with a sharp, sometimes painful, awareness of the world's darker realities.

Her first real mission came at eighteen, when she was tasked with attending a high-profile social event hosted by a suspected arms dealer. Her role was simple: observe, record, and transmit. It was there she first tasted the intoxicating rush of adrenaline—the thrill of living on the precipice of danger. It was also during this mission that she first encountered the blend of power and peril that would define her adult life.

Her ability to infiltrate high society with ease, coupled with her sharp intellect and remarkable memory, made her an invaluable asset to Mossad. They cultivated her, honing her skills until she became a weapon—one they wielded without hesitation. She excelled, moving from social infiltration to more physically demanding tasks. Her skills expanded, but so did the erosion of her moral compass. She justified the betrayals, the compromises, telling herself she was fighting for a cause she believed in.

As the years wore on, the lines blurred. The cause became less clear; the justifications, more hollow. The missions grew morally ambiguous, the consequences dire. She became embroiled in covert operations spanning continents, involving high-ranking officials and powerful figures. She'd seen things that would haunt her forever—things she could never speak of, even now.

Then came Sharon—everything she wasn't: reckless, impulsive, fiercely independent. Their relationship was a whirlwind of passionate encounters and clandestine meetings.

They shared a bond forged in the fires of danger, a mutual understanding of the dark world they inhabited. Yet, even with him, she found herself holding back, protecting parts of her past too painful to reveal.

Their affair, like so many things in her life, was marked by both intense passion and brutal betrayals. Sharon's actions—especially his violent assault on her—were stark reminders that even those she loved were capable of immense cruelty. It was a watershed moment, forcing her to confront the darkness that had consumed her, to question the choices she had made, the life she had led.

Her cooperation with Detective Pickens was born of guilt, fear, and a desperate desire for redemption. She was tired of the lies, the manipulations, the constant threat of exposure. She longed for atonement, for a measure of peace, even if it meant facing the consequences of her past mistakes.

The betrayal of Sharon, though painful, was not unexpected. She had known the risks—he was a loose cannon, prone to unpredictable bursts of violence. Their time together, intense as it was, had never promised stability or commitment, given their professions and their history.

Her tale ended with a chilling revelation: a clandestine meeting in a shadowy Marrakech riad, where she encountered a figure from her past—an abandoned Mossad handler—who revealed that her life had been nothing more than a meticulously constructed illusion. Her past was not her own; it had been a carefully orchestrated pawn in a much larger game.

The story she shared was not just a personal chronicle, but a meditation on the nature of power—the seductive allure and corrosive effects. It was about compromises made, moral lines crossed, and the ultimate price one pays for existing in the shadows. Her tale was a tapestry woven with threads of betrayal, deception, and the chilling realization that, in the world of espionage, the lines between right and wrong, hero and villain, often become hopelessly blurred.

The clinking ice in her glass seemed to underscore the fragility of her existence, the tenuous hold she had on her own sanity. The gaslight flickered once more, casting her face in fleeting darkness, leaving me to wonder just how much of the truth she had shared, and how much remained buried deep within her heart—a secret guarded with the same tenacity and ruthlessness she had learned in the unforgiving world of international espionage. Her past was a labyrinth of deceit and danger, and even now, as she sought a new beginning, the shadows of her past continued to reach out, threatening to engulf her once more.

The Israeli Mobs Structure

The Moroccan sun blazed down on the dusty streets of Casablanca, casting a sharp contrast to the cool, shadowy interiors of the cafes where the Israeli mob conducted its covert dealings. Miriam's story had unlocked a door—a crack in the wall that separated my limited understanding from the brutal, hidden world beneath. Her past, intertwined with the Mossad and now tangled with this shadowy organization, held the key to unraveling the Israeli mob's operations in Morocco. It wasn't a monolithic entity, a singular boss issuing orders from a gilded throne; it was far more intricate—a web of families, clans, and independent operators, all scrambling for power and profit, united only by their shared ethnicity and a willingness to bend—or break—any rule to achieve their goals.

The structure, I discovered, was not hierarchical but rhizomatic—a sprawling network of interconnected nodes, where power shifted and alliances formed and dissolved with the fluidity of desert sands. At its core were the "families," often extended kinship groups that had migrated from Israel, carrying with them their tribal loyalties and a strict sense of omertà—the code of silence. These weren't mere petty criminals; they controlled major sectors of the Moroccan economy, from real estate and import-export businesses to the lucrative diamond trade and, of course, the drug trafficking networks stretching across the Mediterranean.

Within each family, power wasn't necessarily inherited but earned through a ruthless mix of cunning and the ability to cultivate loyalty. The head of a family, the "Patriarch," wasn't always the eldest or most charismatic, but the one who commanded the most respect—or fear. His authority was solidified through an intricate web of relationships, enforced by a brutal system of rewards and punishments. Betrayal was met with swift, often violent retribution.

But the families weren't isolated. They interacted, sometimes cooperating on large-scale operations, other times fiercely competing for territory and resources. These relationships were ever-shifting, dictated by mutual advantage and personal ambition. This fluidity made the network difficult to infiltrate or dismantle. A seemingly minor dispute could trigger a bloody turf war, while an unbreakable alliance could crumble in an instant.

Above the families, though not always directly controlling them, were the "syndicates"—loosely connected groups often composed of representatives from various families. They coordinated larger-scale operations and settled disputes between factions. Acting as an informal governing body, they set guidelines—admittedly, only loosely adhered to—and mediated conflicts to prevent open gang warfare that would attract unwanted attention from Moroccan authorities, or, potentially, Israeli intelligence.

This lack of centralized leadership was both the mob's strength and its greatest vulnerability. The decentralized nature made it resilient to law enforcement: taking down one family didn't dismantle the whole operation; it simply shifted the balance of power, creating new opportunities for ambitious players. Yet this same structure also sowed internal friction and created openings for betrayal. The constant jockeying for power, the rivalries, the backstabbing—these were the cracks that could ultimately bring the whole empire crumbling down.

Beyond the families and syndicates were the "freelancers"— independent operators who worked for the highest bidder. They carried out the most perilous tasks—assassinations, kidnappings, extortion—and were expendable elements in the mob's ecosystem. Hired guns without the loyalty or protection afforded to family members, their lives were valued for their skills, yet often ended violently. They thrived or died by their reputation, knowing that one misstep could cost them everything.

The Israeli mob in Morocco also maintained close ties with other criminal organizations, both locally and internationally. They collaborated with Italian mafias, Colombian cartels, and other groups, forging alliances based on mutual interests and shared benefits. These international connections allowed them to expand their reach, diversify income sources, and launder money through complex offshore accounts and shell corporations. Their influence extended far beyond the dusty streets of Casablanca, infiltrating the very heart of global finance.

The flow of money—the lifeblood of the operation—moved through a labyrinth of shell companies, offshore accounts, and cash transactions. Much of the wealth generated from their illicit activities was laundered through legitimate businesses, hiding its origins. Real estate investments, import-export businesses, even respectable charities—each served as a front for moving dirty money. Tracing these funds was a nightmare, a task requiring meticulous investigation and deep knowledge of international finance.

Equally critical was the violence that underpinned the organization. It wasn't just a tool for resolving disputes; it was a means of maintaining control, instilling fear, and enforcing the code of silence. Assassinations were a regular occurrence, carried out with ruthless efficiency. The victims were usually those who betrayed the mob, threatened its operations, or simply crossed the wrong person. The ever-present threat of violence served as a constant reminder of the consequences of disloyalty or defiance.

In my investigation of the Israeli mob, I found an organization that was both complex and brutal. Its structure, fluid yet resilient, made it difficult to target, but internal rivalries and ambitions created cracks that could be exploited. The mob's international ties enabled it to operate with relative impunity, laundering its gains through an intricate web of financial transactions. Understanding this structure was essential to understanding the true cost of power—the price of living in the shadows—and the dangerous game that Miriam and I were now both entangled in.

The price, as Miriam's story had so clearly illustrated, was steep. It was measured not just in lives lost and fortunes amassed, but in the erosion of one's soul—the slow decay of morality, the constant gnawing fear of betrayal. It was a price she had paid, and one that I was now starting to comprehend. The world of espionage and organized crime was not a battlefield of clear lines and defined enemies. It was a murky swamp where alliances shifted like quicksand, and the only constant was the unrelenting pursuit of power—a pursuit that often led to the ultimate price: the loss of everything.

What Miriam revealed went far beyond the immediate threat of the Israeli mob. It pointed to a larger, far more insidious network of corruption, a system where state power, organized crime, and international intelligence blurred into a volatile mixture. The implications for global security were staggering, and the potential for violence and chaos was vast. This wasn't just about bringing down a criminal organization—it was about exposing a deeply-rooted system of corruption that threatened to destabilize entire regions.

My own history with the Mossad, the betrayal I had suffered, added a layer of complexity. I was no longer an outsider watching from the periphery; I was deeply enmeshed in this web of deceit and danger. The stakes were higher than ever, and the consequences of failure—unimaginable.

The investigation ahead would demand more than just brute force; it required strategic finesse. It meant piecing together fragmented information, interpreting cryptic messages, and navigating the treacherous terrain of international diplomacy and organized crime. It meant confronting my own demons— the ghosts of past mistakes and betrayals—and grappling with the lingering doubt of whether I could trust anyone. The path ahead was perilous, fraught with danger at every turn, but the need to expose the truth and dismantle this sprawling criminal network was a responsibility I couldn't ignore. The price of inaction, I knew, would be far greater than the risk involved in confronting the darkness that had taken root in the heart of Casablanca. The game had begun, and the stakes had never been higher.

The Muslim Brotherhoods Intrigue

The whispers began softly, like the rustling of desert winds through the date palms. At first, they were dismissed as nothing more than the typical paranoia of the Israeli mob, but the rumors of a Brotherhood cell operating within their ranks grew louder, more insistent. This wasn't about petty theft or internal squabbles; it was something far more sinister—an infiltration with the goal of dismantling their operations from within. The whispers spoke of coded messages, secret meetings in the labyrinthine souks of Casablanca, and the sudden, unexplained disappearances of key figures in the organization. My informants—an eclectic group I'd cultivated over years of working in the shadows—confirmed the unsettling truth. The Brotherhood wasn't just trying to establish a foothold; they were angling to control the flow of illicit funds, weapons, and drugs that fueled the mob's operations.

My investigation led me to a seemingly inconspicuous import-export business, a front for a sophisticated money-laundering scheme. The owner, Omar, was a devout Muslim, known for his piety and generosity within the local community. His outward appearance concealed a ruthless pragmatism—an opportunistic willingness to exploit religion for political and financial gain, characteristic of the Brotherhood's strategy. Omar's generosity was a calculated move, buying loyalty and silencing dissent, a subtle form of control that extended beyond the confines of his business. As my investigation deepened, it became clear that Omar was just a pawn in a much larger game—an intermediary for funds flowing from the Brotherhood's global network to support their covert activities within Morocco. The money wasn't simply being laundered; it was being strategically deployed to corrupt officials, manipulate elections, and sow discord within Morocco's already volatile social fabric.

The more I uncovered, the more I realized the Brotherhood's sophistication. They weren't operating in isolation. Their network reached deep into Morocco's government, with corrupt officials turning a blind eye to their activities in exchange for a share of the profits or promises of future political power. This intricate web of complicity extended beyond national borders, stretching into the tangled corridors of international finance and diplomacy. The scale of the Brotherhood's operation was breathtaking—far exceeding anything I had encountered in my previous dealings with organized crime.

One night, following a lead from a jittery informant, I witnessed a clandestine meeting in the dimly lit basement of a mosque. The air was heavy with the scent of incense and hushed whispers. The meeting was shrouded in secrecy, its participants cloaked in shadows, their faces only partially obscured. I watched as Omar, flanked by two other men, engaged in a tense discussion. Their voices were low, barely audible, as they meticulously counted stacks of cash, recording transactions in a worn leather-bound ledger. The ledger, I would later discover, contained a detailed account of the Brotherhood's financial activities—a roadmap to their vast network of operatives and collaborators. It was a treasure trove of information, a key to unlocking the secrets of their operation, and potentially a weapon that could bring down their entire enterprise.

Securing the ledger would be no small feat. I knew that obtaining it would mean confronting the Brotherhood directly, putting my life in jeopardy. The risk was substantial, but the potential reward—exposing the network and disrupting their operations—was too significant to ignore.

The opportunity came during a chaotic power outage, which plunged the mosque into darkness. Using the cover of the blackout, I slipped into the basement and retrieved the ledger, vanishing into the labyrinthine alleys of Casablanca. The streets were my allies that night, guiding me through the maze-like corridors, and disappearing into the shadows.

The ledger, however, was more than just a record of names and figures. It was a window into the Brotherhood's strategic thinking, revealing their long-term goals and their intricate plans for infiltrating the Moroccan government. Their ambitions stretched far beyond Morocco's borders. The implications were far-reaching and deeply unsettling. The meticulously kept records detailed strategies for influencing elections, infiltrating key government ministries, and establishing sleeper cells across Europe and North America.

Analyzing the ledger, I discovered a sophisticated system of coded messages and encrypted communication channels. Each entry held multiple layers of meaning, revealing the Brotherhood's precise planning and operational efficiency. Their infiltration wasn't haphazard—it was a carefully orchestrated campaign, executed with surgical precision. The network extended deep into political figures, business leaders, and even law enforcement. Their presence wasn't a mere nuisance; it was a deep-seated threat to the integrity of the Moroccan government and broader regional stability. The information within the ledger was a chilling revelation.

The records painted a disturbing picture of the Brotherhood's ambition to reshape the political landscape of the region. Their influence reached far beyond simple corruption and money laundering. They were orchestrating political manipulation with long-term goals of establishing a powerful Islamist state. This wasn't just organized crime—it was a threat to national security with international ramifications.

The scale of the operation was staggering. The Brotherhood's network extended far beyond Morocco, encompassing operatives, sympathizers, and collaborators in multiple countries. This made dismantling the organization a complicated task that would require international cooperation and a multi-pronged approach.

My work wasn't over. Far from it. The ledger provided a roadmap, but navigating its complexities would require a delicate balance—exposing the Brotherhood while protecting my own identity. The price of power, I was beginning to understand, was far higher than I'd ever imagined. It wasn't just measured in money; it was paid in lives, betrayals, and the gnawing fear of the unknown. The game, I realized, was far from over. The stakes had never been higher. My past, my betrayals, my choices and regrets—everything was beginning to converge, threatening to engulf me in a tidal wave of consequences. The Moroccan sun was setting, casting long shadows across the city—a fitting metaphor for the darkening reality of my situation. The next move would have to be calculated, precise, and utterly ruthless.

The shadows of Casablanca held their breath, awaiting my next move. The whispers of the Brotherhood had grown into a roaring storm, threatening to engulf the entire region. And I, a mere pawn in this larger game, found myself at its center.

Power Dynamics

The ledger, a meticulously maintained record of the Brotherhood's insidious infiltration, revealed a chilling and intricate web of interconnectedness. This was not the work of a singular, isolated cell; no, it was a hydra, its many heads stretching throughout the Moroccan underworld. Each head, seemingly independent, ultimately served the same dark and sinister purpose. The names listed within the ledger were not those of mere low-level operatives; several of them occupied positions of significant influence within the Israeli mob. Their loyalty had been bought not only through coercion but also through carefully orchestrated bribes. These individuals were far from pawns; they were key players, wielding considerable power within the organization.

Initially, my plan had been straightforward: expose the Brotherhood's sprawling network, dismantle their operations, and walk away with the reward. But the reality I faced was far more complex. The power dynamics at play were intricate and ever-shifting, like the sands of the desert beneath a relentless sun. While the Brotherhood appeared formidable, they were not the only ones with hands on the reins of control. Rival factions within the Israeli mob each vied for dominance, each holding their own agendas and making alliances with anyone who could further their cause. The simple act of exposing the Brotherhood could inadvertently strengthen one faction, undermining another, thus creating a volatile power vacuum that could destabilize the entire region.

Every move I considered had wide-reaching implications. Exposing a single traitor could inadvertently shield another, sparking a chain of unintended consequences. The delicate balance of power—carefully nurtured over decades through bloodshed and deceit—now hung precariously in the balance. One wrong move could ignite a catastrophic chain reaction, plunging not only the Moroccan underworld but the entire region into chaos.

My contacts within Mossad—those few who still remained loyal to me—offered conflicting advice. Some urged caution, advocating for a gradual and careful dismantling of the Brotherhood's network in an effort to minimize collateral damage. Others pushed for a more aggressive approach, advocating for a swift, decisive strike to eliminate the threat before it could fully consolidate its power.

The division within the Israeli mob mirrored this internal debate. The older guard, those who had built their empires through years of brutal violence, favored a traditional approach: violent retribution. They viewed the Brotherhood as a direct threat to their established order and were prepared to use any means necessary to destroy it. On the other hand, the younger generation, more sophisticated and pragmatic, saw the potential for a profitable alliance, perhaps even a hostile takeover. They viewed the Brotherhood's vast network of connections as an opportunity to expand their influence, opening new avenues for money laundering and arms trafficking. This internal struggle for power was perhaps the most dangerous element of all, creating a volatile environment rife with uncertainty and betrayal. Navigating this minefield required finesse, as every step I took risked triggering an explosive chain of events.

Amid this turmoil, one figure stood out: Yakov "The Serpent" Levi, the aging patriarch of the Israeli mob in Casablanca. His position was precarious. While he was respected for his ruthlessness, his unpredictable temperament made him a volatile and dangerous leader. Shrewd and calculating, he understood the intricacies of power dynamics and was a master of manipulation. Yet, age had begun to erode his grip on power, and his authority was increasingly challenged by younger, more ambitious rivals within his own ranks. Yakov was aware of the Brotherhood's infiltration, but his response was cautious, almost paralyzed by indecision. Trapped between his desire to maintain his hold on power and the fear of provoking a conflict that could shatter his empire, he found himself in a precarious position.

My relationship with Yakov was complicated—marked by both mutual respect and simmering resentment. He had once been my mentor, guiding me through the brutal world of espionage and organized crime. But over time, our paths had diverged. Our goals were no longer aligned, and now, his valuable information—critical to exposing the Brotherhood's network—came at a steep cost. Extracting it from him would require a delicate balance of manipulation and intimidation. Yakov, the viper, was always poised to strike.

The ledger itself provided only fragments—clues that, when pieced together, offered a clearer picture of the Brotherhood's long-term strategy. Their goal wasn't merely to infiltrate the Israeli mob; they were manipulating the flow of illicit funds, drugs, and weapons, channeling them toward their own global objectives. Their network extended far beyond Morocco, reaching into the United States, with the ultimate aim of destabilizing Western governments and economies. This was no longer just a local conflict—it was part of a much larger, global chess game, with the Brotherhood playing a dangerously unpredictable role.

My own position in this complex web of power was tenuous at best. As a double agent, I was playing both sides, maneuvering within the currents of conflicting loyalties. My past actions, my betrayals, cast a long shadow over my current circumstances. The Mossad saw me as a liability, a loose cannon that needed to be neutralized. The Israeli mob viewed me as a valuable asset, but also as someone whose loyalty was always in question. And the Brotherhood? They remained blissfully unaware of my true intentions.

The nights in Casablanca were long, filled with the vibrant sounds of the city—the cries of street vendors, the hum of distant traffic, the whispered conversations in darkened alleyways. Each night brought with it new challenges, new betrayals, new threats. The weight of the information I carried was overwhelming, a heavy burden that I couldn't shake. Every move I made was fraught with danger, and every decision carried the potential for catastrophic consequences. I was beginning to realize that the price of power wasn't merely measured in money or influence; it was measured in lives, in betrayals, and in the constant fear of exposure. The ever-present threat of being caught in the crossfire was something I lived with daily.

This game, far from being over, was only just beginning. The final move would not only determine my fate, but also the fate of many others trapped in this deadly conspiracy. The shadows of Casablanca held their breath, waiting for what would come next. And I, trapped in the heart of this storm, waited with them. The game was a delicate balance, and one wrong move could send everything spiraling into chaos. The city itself—a breathtaking blend of beauty and darkness—was a perfect reflection of the conflict raging inside me. The stakes had never been higher.

The Consequences of Corruption

The ledger, a chilling testament to the Brotherhood's insidious reach, lay open before me. Its pages, filled with meticulously crafted code names and carefully disguised transactions, detailed a conspiracy that stretched far beyond the dusty streets of Casablanca. The names whispered secrets of influence peddling, of government officials compromised, their allegiances bought and sold like cheap trinkets in a souk. The sheer scale of it was breathtaking, terrifying. This was not simply about money; it was about power—power of a magnitude that could topple governments and reshape the very geopolitics of the Middle East. A power that had its tendrils wrapped tightly around the heart of the American political system, threading its way into every corner of influence.

As I absorbed the magnitude of this revelation, I realized that the consequences were far-reaching, extending far beyond the immediate players involved. The seemingly insignificant bribes, the inconsequential favors, had created a vast and deeply entrenched network of dependency and complicity, where loyalty itself had become a commodity, traded in the dark corners of backroom deals. What had once seemed like a series of small, isolated transactions now appeared as the foundation of a deep-rooted and systemic rot that threatened the very fabric of governance, not just in Morocco, but on a global scale.

This wasn't just about individuals; it was a systemic decay, gnawing at the very core of the Moroccan government—and, more alarmingly, the American one as well. The vulnerability of democratic institutions, exposed by this infiltration, horrified me. The carefully cultivated trust, the supposed checks and balances that had long been the bedrock of both nations' political systems, had proven to be fragile and easily manipulated by those willing to play the long game. Those patient enough to worm their way into the most secure corridors of power. The thought that such structures could be so easily dismantled, distorted, and controlled by an unseen hand was a terrifying realization.

I couldn't help but think of Miriam, her face a ghost in the dim light of my memory. Her betrayal, her brutal assault, was a direct consequence of this same insidious corruption. She, too, had been caught in the crossfire—a pawn in a larger game that she could not fully comprehend. Her life had been shattered by the reckless ambition of those above her, and her story echoed across the ledger's pages, a microcosm of the larger tragedy unfolding around me. The price she had paid was steep, and it stirred a surge of bitter guilt, a taste of responsibility I could not escape.

But the truth was, my own involvement was inextricably tied to this web of deceit. My past actions, my fall into the criminal underworld, had made me a participant in this corrupt ecosystem. The lines between right and wrong, between justice and revenge, had long since blurred, leaving me adrift in a moral quagmire of my own making. I had traded my ideals for survival, my integrity for a fleeting sense of power. And now, the consequences of those choices loomed over me like a suffocating weight I could barely endure.

The ledger revealed a pattern, a disturbingly consistent method of infiltration. The Brotherhood had not relied on brute force; instead, they had cultivated relationships, strategically placed bribes, and exploited vulnerabilities in ways that left no trace. They moved slowly, patiently, like a venomous snake slithering through tall grass. They identified their targets among the ambitious, the desperate, the morally compromised—those who could be easily seduced by the promise of power and wealth. And in doing so, they exploited the existing fractures within society—those simmering feelings of resentment and disillusionment—to sow seeds of discord and achieve their ultimate goals.

The Moroccan government, already weakened by years of instability, rampant inequality, and endemic corruption, was particularly vulnerable. The Brotherhood had recognized the fault lines in the system, identifying individuals who were susceptible to manipulation, and expertly leveraged their vulnerabilities. They had not merely infiltrated the government; they had essentially bought it—bribing officials at every level, from minor clerks to high-ranking ministers. The implications of this were staggering. The country's security apparatus was compromised, its laws rendered meaningless, and its sovereignty hanging by a thread.

But the infiltration didn't stop at Morocco's borders. The ledger hinted at an even wider conspiracy, one that reached into the very heart of American politics. The names and dates referenced clandestine meetings, coded communications, and covert operations—each entry another chilling step in a larger plan. The thought of a successful infiltration of the US government sent a shiver down my spine. Such a move would have catastrophic consequences, not only destabilizing the region but threatening the very fabric of American democracy itself. The ripple effects would be felt across the world, and the chaos that would follow was unimaginable.

For nights on end, I poured over the ledger, piecing together the fragmented puzzle. The sheer scale of the conspiracy was overwhelming. It was not a single, isolated incident—it was a meticulously planned operation, spanning years and involving countless individuals. And it had one ultimate objective: to destabilize the region and exert influence over American foreign policy. The Brotherhood's patience was nothing short of remarkable. They were not interested in quick victories; their strategy was long-term, insidious, and devastatingly effective.

The thought of the potential damage chilled me to the bone.

The consequences of this corruption were not limited to financial losses or political instability; they extended to human lives—lives lost in acts of terrorism, lives destroyed by betrayal and violence. If their plans went unchecked, the death toll would rise exponentially.

The gravity of the situation could not have been clearer. This wasn't simply a case of corruption; it was a profound threat to global security. The consequences would ripple outward, touching everything and everyone. The impact of their actions was far-reaching, causing families to be torn apart, careers ruined, and the very foundation of trust shattered. The psychological damage was immeasurable. The erosion of faith in institutions would be a wound that could take generations to heal.

I had to find a way to stop them. But how? The odds seemed insurmountable. The Brotherhood had deep roots, powerful allies, and an almost limitless supply of money. Taking them down would require not only skill, cunning, and experience but also a measure of luck and, perhaps most critically, an immense amount of courage. I was no longer a Mossad agent— I was a hunted man, a criminal, a pariah. But I knew I could not stand idly by while these men threatened the world.

My past—the mistakes, the violence, and the betrayals I had inflicted—haunted me like ghosts that refused to rest. But I couldn't afford to dwell on them. I had a job to do. My knowledge, my skills, my experience in the criminal underworld had prepared me for this moment. To do nothing would be to betray everything I once stood for, to condemn countless others to the same fate as Miriam. The price of power, I was beginning to understand, was far greater than I had ever imagined. And I was prepared to pay it, whatever the cost, to ensure that justice—however delayed—would eventually prevail.

The consequences of inaction were far too horrifying to contemplate. The weight of the world, and the responsibility for my actions, now fell squarely on my shoulders. The game, far from being over, had only just begun. And now, it had become infinitely more dangerous.

Cohens Imprisonment

The steel door slammed shut with a resounding clang, its reverberation echoing through the sterile hallways—a harsh, final punctuation to Cohen's downfall. The sterile hum of fluorescent lights above cut through the quiet like a constant reminder of his confinement. The adrenaline that had once coursed through his veins now left him in an uneasy calm, a strange quiet that filled the empty space between the walls of his holding cell. He'd expected a fight, a last desperate stand against the inevitable, yet there had been only the chilling embrace of acceptance as the cold metal cuffs clicked into place around his wrists.

The defiance that had fueled his reckless years of power and excess had finally dissipated, replaced by a bone-deep weariness. It was as though the years of reckless abandon had drained him of his vigor, leaving him hollow and exhausted.

The first few days passed in a blur of sensory deprivation, the rough concrete walls and the oppressive stillness a cruel contrast to the luxurious hotels and smoky backrooms that had once been his domain. The stale air in the cell was suffocating, the constant clang of metal doors in the distance a stark reminder of his new reality. The other inmates, a motley collection of hardened criminals, regarded him with a mixture of curiosity and disdain. He was the ghost of Marrakech, a name whispered in dark corners of the underworld, spoken in tones laced with fear and respect. Yet here, stripped of his power, reduced to nothing more than a number, he was as vulnerable as any man.

He adapted quickly, learning the unspoken rules of this new world, the currency of favors, grudges, and alliances that governed every interaction behind the prison walls. He was a chameleon by nature, a master of adapting to his surroundings, and in this brutal environment, that skill became his survival mechanism. He kept his head down, observing and listening, careful not to attract attention while plotting his next move.

He steered clear of the obvious gangs and the tribal affiliations that dominated the prison's pecking order. Instead, he found a strange solace in the prison library, devouring books on history, philosophy, even poetry. It was a form of self-imposed exile, a retreat into the world of ideas to escape the harsh reality of his situation. The books, though a temporary escape, became a lifeline, a bridge to a past he could no longer return to, but a part of himself he could still nurture.

His interactions with the other inmates were minimal, measured, and always calculated. He shared cigarettes with a grizzled veteran, a former soldier who understood the burden of violence. He exchanged terse words with a young man—a petty thief, whose haunted eyes betrayed the weight of regret that carried the past of many. He learned their stories, their vulnerabilities, and motivations, even offering advice from time to time—a strange turn of fate for a man who had once lived his life exploiting others for his own gain. It was a subtle shift, a crack in the hardened shell he had cultivated over years of deception and bloodshed. For the first time in a long while, he was no longer the predator; he was the prey. And though humbling, it was a role that felt, in some ways, long overdue.

Among the prisoners, one man, in particular, piqued Cohen's interest—a wiry man named Omar. Omar was a political prisoner, a journalist who had dared to expose corruption within the Moroccan government. Their conversations were few, fleeting moments snatched in the prison yard, but each one revealed a shared understanding of betrayal and the weight of political intrigue. Omar's quiet dignity, his unshakable belief in justice even within these oppressive walls, began to chip away at the cynicism Cohen had buried deep within himself. He began to see glimpses of his younger self in Omar, a man once driven by idealism, a part of him that had been buried beneath layers of bitterness and violence.

Life in the prison settled into a monotonous rhythm—wake, eat, work, sleep, repeat. Cohen found work in the prison kitchen, blending into the background, observing, and plotting. But he wasn't plotting an escape—not yet, at least. Instead, he was slowly dismantling the walls that had once confined him. He used his charm, his sharp intellect, and his cunning to forge alliances, to gather information, to build trust. He was no longer playing the same high-stakes game he had once known, the game of brute force and manipulation. This was a quieter, subtler game, one that required patience and long-term thinking. And Cohen was nothing if not patient.

Then, one day, a new inmate arrived—young, barely a man, his haunted eyes betraying a pain beyond his years. He was the son of a wealthy Israeli businessman, a victim of a kidnapping gone wrong. The whispers that circulated in the common room were vague, but Cohen recognized the pattern—a contract killing, eerily similar to the ones he had orchestrated in the past. A sickening sense of familiarity washed over him, and for the first time in years, Cohen felt something stir deep inside him—guilt. He saw in this young man a reflection of his younger self, a man whose innocence had been shattered by the same world that had swallowed Cohen whole.

Despite his hardened exterior, Cohen felt compelled to protect the young man, offering subtle warnings about the dangers lurking in the prison environment. He shared his meager rations with him, offering a small crumb of comfort in an otherwise bleak and unforgiving landscape. It was a small act, seemingly insignificant in the grand scheme of things, but for Cohen, it felt profound—a shift in his nature, a step toward redemption that, for the first time in years, seemed possible.

But the authorities, ever vigilant, were tightening their grip. They had Cohen, but they wanted more. They wanted information—names, contacts, the full extent of his operations. They tried intimidation, they tried interrogation, but Cohen remained silent, a ghost in their justice system. His silence, he knew, was a weapon. It was his defiance, a final act of resistance against a system he had once served but now despised.

Then came the twist. A high-ranking Mossad official, a man Cohen had once respected, visited him in prison with an offer—a deal. In exchange for information, Cohen would be granted freedom, immunity, a fresh start. But this wasn't about Al-Qaeda or the Muslim Brotherhood. This was bigger—far bigger. The conspiracy reached into the highest echelons of power, touching international banking, arms dealing, and possibly even the US government itself.

Cohen's mind raced. This was a game-changer. He had been a pawn, a tool, but now, suddenly, he was being offered a chance to become a player. Power. Influence. A chance to rewrite the narrative of his life. The offer was tempting, the carrot dangling in front of him like a prize. But Cohen knew all too well the price of betrayal, the cost of choosing one side over another. He had been a player in this game before, and he knew the consequences of playing both sides.

He knew the hand of fate was offering him a new card, full of dangerous possibilities. But what would he choose? One thing was certain: this game was far from over. It had only just begun.

A Twist of Fate

The stale air of the holding cell pressed against Cohen like a physical weight. He stared at the peeling paint on the wall, the chipped concrete floor a grim reminder of his fall from grace. The silence, broken only by the rhythmic hum of the fluorescent lights, was more unnerving than any shouting match or physical altercation. He'd faced death countless times, but this quiet anticipation was a different kind of torment. It was the waiting, the uncertainty, that gnawed at him.

Then, the door rattled. A guard, his face impassive, slid a tray of food through the slot. Standard fare: a tasteless sandwich, a bruised apple, a lukewarm cup of coffee. Cohen ignored it, his gaze fixed on the door. He knew this wasn't a routine food delivery.

The guard returned, this time accompanied by a man in a sharply tailored suit. He was clean-shaven, his hair neatly combed, and his demeanor radiated an air of controlled power. He didn't introduce himself, just sat down on the small metal stool opposite Cohen.

"Mr. Cohen," the man began, his voice a low, smooth baritone, "we have a proposition for you."

Cohen remained silent, his eyes narrowed. He'd dealt with enough shadowy figures in his life to recognize the subtle shift in the air—the unspoken threat underlying the polite words.

"Your arrest," the man continued, "wasn't entirely... straightforward. Let's just say there were... certain irregularities in the procedure." He paused, letting the implication linger in the air. "We believe you possess information of considerable value."

Cohen chuckled, a dry, brittle sound. "Value? To whom? The Mossad? The Israeli mob? Or perhaps... the Americans?"

The man smiled faintly. "Let's just say it's a matter of national security. Information that could prevent a catastrophic event. We are offering you a chance to cooperate, to help us avert a disaster."

"And what's in it for me?" Cohen asked, his tone laced with skepticism.

"A new identity," the man replied. "A clean slate. A chance to start over. Far away from here. From your past."

Cohen considered this. A clean slate? The irony wasn't lost on him. He'd built his life on erasing his past, shedding identities like a snake sheds its skin. This offer was a twisted mirror image of his previous life—a chance to rewrite the script, to escape the inevitable consequences of his actions.

"What kind of information are we talking about?" Cohen asked, his voice betraying a flicker of interest.

The man leaned closer, his voice dropping to a whisper. "It concerns a cell within the Muslim Brotherhood, far more insidious and dangerous than the one you were originally tasked with infiltrating. They're deeply embedded within the US government, working towards a goal that could destabilize the entire region."

This was new. This was beyond anything Cohen had encountered in his career. He'd been involved in conspiracies, betrayals, and murders, but this felt different—a global chess game on a scale he hadn't imagined. His initial skepticism began to wane, replaced by a chilling fascination.

"And if I refuse?" Cohen asked, testing the waters.

The man's smile vanished. "Then you'll face the full weight of the law. And let's be honest, Mr. Cohen, your past is hardly a testament to your adherence to legality."

The implication hung heavily in the air: solitary confinement, a lengthy trial, the prospect of spending the rest of his days behind bars. He knew they weren't bluffing.

The hours that followed were a blur of hushed conversations, carefully worded questions, and cryptic answers. Cohen, the master manipulator, found himself being manipulated. He played his part, feeding them snippets of information, withholding crucial details, testing the boundaries of their offer. He was a caged animal, but even a caged animal can strike.

He learned about the cell's intricate network, their connections to powerful figures within the US government, their plans to exploit existing tensions to create widespread chaos. He learned about their complex financial dealings, the coded messages, and the hidden agendas. He learned that this operation went far beyond the initial Al-Qaeda bombing plot. This was a far bigger game, involving players far more powerful and influential than he could have ever imagined.

As the interrogation progressed, a grudging respect began to develop between Cohen and his interrogator. The man understood power, understood leverage, understood the language of espionage. He saw the glint of intellect in Cohen's eyes, the sharp mind behind the hardened exterior.

They were two sides of the same coin—masters of deception, players in a deadly game.

Finally, as dawn broke, painting the prison walls in pale gray light, Cohen agreed. He would cooperate. He would help them dismantle the cell. But he had his own conditions, his own demands. He wasn't just a pawn; he would be a player, dictating the terms of his involvement, ensuring that his cooperation was not a one-way street.

He insisted on immunity from prosecution, a new identity, and substantial financial compensation. He demanded complete control over his interactions with the authorities, a shield against betrayal. He was walking a tightrope, negotiating with the very people who had once sought to destroy him. Yet, he had leverage. He possessed information that could shake the foundations of the American government. He would use this information not only to secure his own freedom but to reshape his destiny. The hand of fate had dealt him a cruel blow, but he was not one to surrender. He would play the hand he'd been dealt, and he would win. His survival, his redemption, hinged on this perilous gamble. The game, far from being over, was only just beginning.

His new life wouldn't be easy. He knew there would be risks, betrayals, and further bloodshed. But the prospect of a clean slate, of leaving his violent past behind, was too alluring to resist. He had a score to settle—not only with the Muslim Brotherhood cell, but with the forces that had betrayed him within the Mossad and the Israeli underworld. He would use this chance to dismantle the network that had orchestrated his downfall. He would use their weapons against them. This wasn't just a matter of survival; this was his revenge. His twisted sense of justice, honed through years of deception and violence, would guide him. And this time, he would be playing by his own rules. The unexpected twist of fate had presented him with a chance not only to survive but to thrive. His chess game had just started.

New Threats Emerge

The fluorescent hum of the holding cell persisted, a monotonous drone that seemed to echo Cohen's simmering rage. He'd expected a brutal interrogation, perhaps even a physical confrontation with his captors. Instead, he was confronted with a chilling silence—one that spoke volumes about the power dynamics at play. Cohen knew his capture wasn't the end of the story; it was merely the opening act of a much larger, far more complex game.

Days melted into one another, a blur of bland meals, sporadic interrogations that yielded little of consequence, and the ever-looming weight of his past sins. His mind, a battlefield of memories and strategies, worked relentlessly, dissecting every interaction and every subtle shift in the guards' demeanor. He searched for weaknesses, cracks in the system he could exploit. It wasn't a matter of if he'd escape, but when and how.

Then came the whispers—not the blatant threats or accusations, but hushed conversations in the corridors, furtive glances exchanged between guards, almost imperceptible changes in routine. A new threat was emerging, one far more menacing than the usual prison politics. A shadow lurked at the edge of his confinement.

It began subtly—slight tremors in the ground, barely perceptible at first, then growing stronger with each passing day. Initially, he dismissed them, attributing them to the city's usual seismic activity. But the tremors soon became accompanied by a low, guttural hum—a vibration that reverberated deep within his bones, a feeling that hinted at something far more sinister than a natural occurrence. The guards, once indifferent, began to behave strangely—more jittery, their movements sharper, their eyes constantly scanning the surroundings.

One evening, a seasoned guard approached Cohen's cell, his face etched with worry and exhaustion. In hushed tones, he whispered, "They're coming. Something... something big. It's not just about you anymore." His cryptic words were enough for Cohen to understand that his case, initially a routine apprehension of a high-profile criminal, had become part of something much larger, more dangerous. The tremors, the hum, the guards' fear—all pointed to a brewing storm, far greater than any force he had previously faced. The Israeli mob, the Muslim Brotherhood cell, the Mossad—insignificant pawns now in a game of a far grander scale.

The following days were a blur of frantic activity. The once calm prison now resembled a warzone. Armed guards patrolled the halls, weapons drawn. Helicopters circled overhead, their blades slicing through the night sky. The news reported strange seismic activity, dismissing it as an unusual geological event, but Cohen knew better.

Then, the earth shook violently. The walls of his cell cracked, the concrete floor buckled. The hum crescendoed into a deafening roar that threatened to shatter his eardrums. Panic erupted. Guards screamed orders, inmates rioted, and the very structure of the prison seemed on the verge of collapse.

In the midst of the chaos, Cohen saw his opportunity. The tremors had weakened a section of the wall near his cell. Armed with a loose piece of concrete, he battered at the weakened wall, creating a narrow opening. He squeezed through the gap, dust and debris stinging his eyes, and found himself thrust into the heart of the pandemonium.

He navigated the madness, utilizing years of training and instinct to remain undetected. Avoiding panicked guards and rioting inmates, his senses heightened and mind focused solely on escape. A service tunnel—dark and claustrophobic—appeared to be his only way out. But Cohen knew that escaping the prison was only the first step. The real battle was just beginning.

Outside, the city was in turmoil. Buildings crumbled, streets were torn apart by fissures in the earth, and the air crackled with an energy that was both terrifying and exhilarating. The hum still reverberated, a constant reminder of the unknown force at play.

Soon, he discovered the source of the tremors and the hum. Deep beneath the city, an ancient, forgotten network of tunnels had been reactivated. An insidious organization, far more powerful and dangerous than anything Cohen had ever encountered, was using the tunnels to deploy a weapon—one capable of causing widespread destruction. As he examined the equipment scattered around the tunnels, Cohen recognized a symbol—one he had seen in ancient texts, associated with a forgotten civilization known for its mastery of earth-shattering technologies.

His capture, his imprisonment—it had all been part of a carefully orchestrated plan. They needed him. His knowledge of the underworld, his understanding of global power dynamics, had made him invaluable. They had used his imprisonment to lure him into their trap.

But Cohen was no longer a pawn. He was a key player in a deadly game. He would not be manipulated. His escape from prison was not just a desperate bid for survival; it was the first move in a much larger, far more dangerous game. The old vendettas—personal betrayals, the Mossad, the Israeli mob, the Muslim Brotherhood—faded into insignificance in the face of a global threat. His past, once a burden, was now a weapon, sharpened by years of pain and conflict.

He would wield it with deadly precision, dismantling the organization that sought to unleash chaos upon the world.

The familiar enemies—Mossad, the Israeli mob, the Muslim Brotherhood cell—now seemed like insignificant players in this new, far more terrifying game. The fate of the world hung precariously in the balance. No longer was Cohen simply fighting for his life. He was fighting for humanity's survival.

The hum continued to reverberate, a constant reminder of the imminent danger. But Cohen, hardened by years of conflict, felt a grim sense of determination settle in. He wasn't afraid. He was ready. The game had changed, and he was poised to play. He was no longer just an ex-Mossad agent, a former criminal, a betrayed lover. He was the only one capable of stopping this looming threat. The weight of the world was on his shoulders, but he bore it with the grim acceptance of a man who had survived worse. Fate had dealt him a cruel hand, but he wasn't one to surrender easily. This time, he would play to win—or die trying. The fight for survival had become a fight for the future of civilization.

And Sharon Cohen, battle-scarred and defiant, would lead the charge.

A Shifting Balance of Power

The silence in the cell was broken only by the rhythmic tick-tock of an unseen clock, a metronome counting down to an unknown event. Cohen, despite his outward composure, felt the pressure mounting. His capture had not triggered the expected storm of accusations and violence. Instead, a chilling calm had settled over his captors—a silence far more ominous than any shouting match. He understood; this was no simple arrest. It was a chess game, and he was but a pawn in a much larger, far more intricate strategy.

His mind raced, piecing together the fragmented clues. The meticulous planning behind the Al-Qaeda operation, the Israeli government's swift removal of gold reserves, his own descent into the criminal underworld—each thread seemed to converge at this singular point. He was a key, and they held the lock. But to what end?

The door clicked open—not the brutal slam he'd anticipated, but a quiet, almost hesitant opening. Two men entered, not the stereotypical interrogators he had imagined, but sharply dressed individuals who seemed more like businessmen than law enforcement. One, a gaunt man with sharp, calculating eyes, carried a leather briefcase. The other, larger and heavier, remained silent, his gaze unwavering.

"Mr. Cohen," the gaunt man began, his voice smooth and precise, a stark contrast to the rough world Cohen inhabited. "We need to talk. About the shifting balance of power."

Cohen remained silent, his gaze fixed on the briefcase. He knew the game was shifting. The initial focus had been on him, his crimes, his past. But now, something far larger was at play.

A sense of foreboding washed over him—a feeling that went beyond his immediate predicament.

The gaunt man continued, unfazed by Cohen's silence. "The events of the past few months have had a profound impact on the geopolitical landscape. The Al-Qaeda attack, the subsequent investigations, your... activities... have all contributed to a delicate realignment. The usual players are no longer in control. New alliances are forming, old loyalties dissolving."

He opened the briefcase, revealing a series of documents, photographs, and intricately detailed maps. Cohen recognized some of the locations: clandestine meeting points in Morocco, safe houses in Dubai, communication channels within the Pakistani underworld. These weren't random pieces of information; they were the intricate threads of a vast web— one he had unwittingly helped to weave.

"We believe you possess information crucial to understanding this new landscape," the gaunt man continued. "Information that could prevent a catastrophic escalation." He paused, letting his words settle. "The Muslim Brotherhood's infiltration of the US government... it's not merely an attempt to destabilize the nation. It's part of a much larger scheme—a power play with global ramifications."

Cohen understood the implications. The Muslim Brotherhood's actions were more than just terrorism; they were a calculated move in a larger game—a strategic gambit to seize control of vital resources and influence. Initially, he had been a pawn in that game, but now, the stakes had changed. He was no longer just a fugitive; he was a potential key to preventing a global catastrophe.

The larger man finally spoke, his voice a low rumble that vibrated through the cell. "We know about your past, Mr. Cohen. Your betrayal, your violence. We also know your skills—your understanding of the Middle East, your intimate knowledge of organized crime, your... ruthlessness."

Cohen met his gaze, a flicker of recognition passing between them. They weren't merely interested in information; they were searching for someone who could navigate this treacherous new world—someone who could play the game and win. A chilling realization dawned on him: They were offering him a deal.

The following days blurred into a whirlwind of negotiations. Cohen, despite his initial defiance, found himself surprisingly receptive. The gaunt man, who identified himself only as "Director," laid out the situation in stark terms. The old order—the established power structures of the Middle East— were crumbling. A complex tapestry of competing interests was filling the vacuum: rogue elements within the Pakistani military, ambitious factions within the Muslim Brotherhood, shadowy international corporations exploiting the chaos for profit, and various intelligence agencies maneuvering for strategic advantage.

Cohen's knowledge, particularly his understanding of the criminal networks operating across the region, proved invaluable. He provided insights into the Brotherhood's funding sources, their alliances with arms dealers, and their infiltration tactics. He explained how they leveraged existing networks of smugglers, corrupt officials, and even religious organizations to achieve their objectives. His insights were chillingly accurate, a testament to his years immersed in the murky world of espionage and crime.

Director listened intently, occasionally making notes in a small, elegant notebook. He acknowledged Cohen's past actions, but his focus remained on his capabilities. He spoke of the shifting alliances, the fragile peace hanging by a thread, and the looming threat of a wider conflict.

"The balance of power is not merely shifting, Mr. Cohen," Director explained, his voice tinged with urgency. "It's collapsing. And only someone with your skills can help us prevent a complete meltdown."

The deal was a gamble—a dangerous dance with the devil. Cohen would assist them in dismantling the Brotherhood's network in the US, providing crucial intelligence and tactical support. In return, they would offer him protection, resources, and the chance to rewrite his history—an opportunity to atone for his past sins by preventing a potentially catastrophic future.

But the deal came with a price. He would have to work with individuals he had once considered enemies: rival intelligence agencies, shadowy figures operating outside the law. The line between right and wrong blurred, and Cohen—a man accustomed to navigating moral gray areas—found himself venturing into terrain more treacherous and morally ambiguous than anything he'd faced before. The game had changed, yes. But the stakes were higher than ever. This wasn't just about survival; it was about the future of the world.

Sharon Cohen, the once-disillusioned Mossad agent and ruthless criminal, found himself once again playing a pivotal role. This time, however, the cards were stacked differently. The hand of fate had dealt him another terrible hand, but now, he held all the aces—or so it seemed. The game had begun anew, with far higher stakes, and Cohen, despite his hardened exterior, felt the tremor of fear mixed with grim determination.

The fight was far from over. The shifting sands of power were still moving, and his next move would determine not only his fate but the fate of the world.

A Glimpse of Redemption

The stale air of the interrogation room clung to him, heavy with the scent of cheap disinfectant and simmering tension. Cohen, stripped of his usual swagger, hunched over a metal table, his reflection a gaunt stranger under the flickering fluorescent light. The silence, once a suffocating blanket, now felt strangely expectant. His captors, a motley crew of Israeli intelligence agents and shadowy figures he wouldn't name even to himself, watched him with a curious mix of suspicion and... something akin to grudging respect.

The offer came unexpectedly, a whisper in the suffocating silence. It wasn't a pardon, not a reprieve, but a proposition—a twisted path toward something resembling redemption.

They laid it out before him, a tangled web of conspiracies and counter-conspiracies, a global chessboard where he, the fallen pawn, could rise to become a knight, a rook, perhaps even a queen.

The target: a clandestine network operating in the shadows of the burgeoning Islamic State, a group plotting an attack on a scale even grander than the World Trade Center bombing. Their leader, a man known only as "The Emir," was pulling strings from a hidden location, orchestrating chaos and bloodshed with chilling efficiency.

Cohen listened, his mind racing, sorting through the layers of deceit and half-truths. He'd played this game before, navigating the treacherous currents of international espionage, but this was different. This felt... personal. The Emir's methods were brutal, his targets often innocent civilians caught in the crossfire of political machinations.

There was a stark contrast to the coldly calculated efficiency of the original Al-Qaeda plot, which, in a strange way, had justified his actions and subsequent descent into darkness.

This, however, was senseless carnage wrapped in a veil of religious zealotry—anathema to him on multiple levels.

The deal, if he could even call it that, wasn't about loyalty or patriotism. It was about preventing a catastrophe, minimizing the inevitable bloodshed. He was being offered a chance to atone for his past sins, not through penance or forgiveness, but through action—through stopping a far greater evil. The price? Collaboration with the very agencies he'd betrayed, a descent into even darker moral ambiguity.

He'd have to work alongside individuals who'd once been rivals, even enemies, playing roles he'd previously scorned. Trust was a luxury he could no longer afford.

The next few days blurred into a whirlwind of clandestine meetings, whispered conversations in dimly lit backrooms, and coded messages exchanged through encrypted channels. He was being debriefed, not as a prisoner, but as an invaluable asset, his unique understanding of both Mossad and the criminal underworld making him indispensable. His past experiences, once a source of shame, had now become a weapon in this new battle. He was forced to confront the ghost of Miriam, his former lover, now a pawn in this larger game of cat and mouse. Both of them danced on the edge of truth and betrayal; the lines blurred and then sharpened once more. Each interaction, each stolen glance, reminded him of his past sins and the present quest for something better.

He was granted access to intelligence files—dossiers on individuals who were both above and below the law. He studied the Emir's operational structure, identifying key figures, vulnerabilities, and predicting his next moves. The process was agonizing, a constant struggle between his inherent cynicism and a newfound sense of purpose. He realized that this act of redemption could only be one of many steps in a journey to cleanse his soul—each victory earned at a great personal cost.

He began to understand the complexity of the operation. This wasn't simply about stopping a terrorist attack; it was about dismantling a deeply entrenched organization with tentacles reaching into governments and criminal networks. He delved into the Emir's funding sources, tracing the flow of illicit money through offshore accounts and shell corporations—a maze of financial transactions that mirrored the intricate web of lies and deceit that had characterized his own past life. He saw how the Emir exploited political instability and religious extremism, using fear and violence to achieve his goals.

The Emir was different than any terrorist Cohen had encountered. Not just another ruthless figure, but a master strategist, playing the long game, manipulating individuals and nations to further his cause. His motives, while brutal and unforgiving, were rooted in an ideology far removed from the petty criminal enterprises of the Israeli mob in Morocco. Cohen saw how easily the Emir's rhetoric could ignite flames of hatred, inciting violence among disillusioned youth—a dangerous echo of the radicalization he'd witnessed during his Mossad days. This wasn't a simple terrorist plot; this was a systematic effort to destabilize the region, sowing chaos, and reaping the rewards of violence.

He spent days analyzing satellite imagery, piecing together fragments of information, confirming his theories and suspicions. The Emir was building a network of sleeper agents, individuals embedded in various communities, waiting for the signal to strike. It was a precise, well-oiled machine, controlled by a man of extraordinary skill. Cohen, with his unique perspective, was crucial to unraveling the puzzle, to find the weak points in the structure, to identify the vulnerable points in the Emir's planning.

His role expanded beyond simple intelligence gathering. He began using his underworld connections to infiltrate the Emir's inner circle. He leveraged his contacts within the Israeli mob, once his colleagues in crime, now reluctant allies. He used his knowledge of Moroccan crime to infiltrate a branch of the network there. The betrayal was a bitter pill to swallow, but it was a necessary evil. His life had been one of deception, and now he used it to fight against a far greater evil. It was a strange form of redemption—an act of counter-terrorism using the tools of the criminal underworld.

The climax arrived in a chaotic showdown in a deserted warehouse on the outskirts of Marrakech, a location that felt both familiar and utterly alien. The Emir, surrounded by his loyal followers, was poised to execute his plan. The battle was fierce—a deadly ballet of bullets and betrayal, a visceral testament to the dark side of humanity, where lines blurred and trust evaporated in the face of violence. It was a reminder of his own violent past, of the pain and suffering he had caused. But this time, his violence was directed at a greater evil, toward saving innocent lives.

In the aftermath, the warehouse lay in ruins, a testament to the brutal struggle. The Emir was gone, his empire crumbling around him. Cohen, battered but alive, had stared into the abyss and emerged victorious—scarred and changed. He had averted a disaster of unimaginable proportions, a victory that would never be formally acknowledged, a redemption won in the shadows. He looked at his hands, still stained with the grime of the underworld, and reflected on the price he'd paid, the moral compromises he'd made, and the long, arduous path toward something he could only vaguely define as peace.

The hand of fate, which had dealt him a cruel blow, had unexpectedly provided him with the opportunity to reclaim his life. No matter how twisted or flawed his redemption, it was his. The game was over, but the scars—both physical and emotional—would remain. He was no longer just Sharon Cohen, the disillusioned Mossad agent or the ruthless criminal. He was something else. Something more complex. Something... redeemed. Or at least, on the path toward it. The long, hard road ahead remained, but he knew, with surprising certainty, that he could finally walk it with his head held just a little higher.

Pickenss Internal Conflict

The fluorescent lights of the precinct hummed a monotonous tune, a harsh counterpoint to the storm brewing inside Tommy Pickens. He stared out the window, the city sprawling before him—a chaotic tapestry of lights and shadows, reflecting the turmoil that churned within. The capture of Sharon Cohen, the ruthless Israeli mobster, should have brought a sense of closure, a victory for justice. Instead, a gnawing unease took root in his gut, a shadow clinging to the edges of his triumph.

Cohen's capture had been anything but clean—a chaotic ballet of gunfire and shattering glass that culminated in a violent standoff in a dilapidated warehouse on the docks. The images still flickered in his mind like a reel of film: Cohen, armed and defiant, eyes wild with madness as he fought tooth and nail against the overwhelming force of the NYPD's SWAT team. The man was a viper—venomous, unpredictable—but even a viper could be caged. Or so Pickens had thought.

What seemed like a closed case continued to unravel in his mind, its threads twisting into an intricate knot of moral ambiguity. He had become entangled, drawn into a world far darker and more complex than he had ever imagined. His relationship with Miriam, Cohen's former lover, had been a double-edged sword—both a source of comfort and a wellspring of conflict. She had been his key, her testimony crucial in bringing Cohen down, but her vulnerability, her haunted eyes speaking volumes of Cohen's cruelty, left him with a heavy heart.

He found himself questioning his methods, the compromises he had made in the name of justice. The line between right and wrong had blurred, slipping away entirely in the murky waters of international espionage and organized crime. He had skirted the edges of legality, pushing boundaries in his dogged pursuit of Cohen. Had he, in his relentless hunt, become something akin to the very monster he was chasing? The question whispered in the back of his mind, persistent and insistent.

The case had exposed the underbelly of New York City—an intricate network of corruption and violence extending far beyond its borders. He had glimpsed the insidious reach of the Israeli mob, the shadowy machinations of the Muslim Brotherhood, and the unsettling involvement of elements within his own government. The more he uncovered, the more he realized how deeply embedded the conspiracy was, and the disturbing realization that Cohen might have been nothing more than a pawn in a far grander game.

Miriam's recovery was slow, arduous. The physical wounds inflicted by Cohen were healing, but the psychological scars ran deeper. He visited her regularly at the safe house, a modest apartment nestled in a quiet neighborhood far removed from the city's bustle. She was like a fragile bird, still trembling from the storm she had weathered, but her spirit, resilient and unwavering, was slowly rekindling. He spent hours listening to her recount her ordeal, her voice a blend of fear and determination. Her testimony had been invaluable, but the cost to her had been immense. Pickens felt an overwhelming sense of responsibility for her well-being, a debt he knew he could never fully repay.

The loose ends continued to gnaw at him. Whispers of Mossad's involvement, unanswered questions surrounding the initial bombing plot, the unsettling mystery of the missing World Trade Center gold. The official narrative had been neatly packaged and presented to the public, but Pickens could sense a deeper truth lurking just beneath the surface. The case felt unfinished, like a symphony missing its final movement.

He spent countless nights poring over the evidence, searching for clues he might have missed. The case files were a labyrinth of names, dates, and locations, a dizzying tapestry of deceit and double-crosses. He often found himself staring at Cohen's mugshot, the man's face a mask of cold calculation. But in those eyes—there was something else. A flicker. Vulnerability, perhaps? Regret? Or was it just a trick of the light?

The question of justice gnawed at him. Had they truly brought Cohen to justice, or had they merely removed a single piece from a far more dangerous puzzle? Cohen's arrest felt like a victory—necessary, but hollow. Beneath the surface, the underlying issues remained unaddressed, a ticking time bomb waiting to detonate. The shadows of the conspiracy stretched long and menacing, unresolved.

The weight of his actions pressed heavily on him. He had compromised his integrity, blurred the lines of his profession, all in the pursuit of a dangerous criminal. But was he truly justified? The answer remained elusive, a phantom he chased through the dark corridors of his own conscience.

He thought of the Pakistani cab drivers murdered by Cohen, their families left to grieve in the shadow of their loss. He thought of the wealthy Israelis, their lives cut short by Cohen's ruthlessness, their families picking up the shattered pieces of their existence. The weight of those lives, those deaths, hung heavily on his shoulders.

Pickens knew that the long shadow of this case would follow him for years to come. The haunting images, the moral questions, the unanswered mysteries would linger—an ever-present reminder of the darkness he had encountered and the compromises he had made. The city lights outside his window dimmed, the shadows growing longer, darker, as he grappled with the moral ambiguities of his pursuit of justice.

The case had been solved—Cohen was behind bars—but the victory felt hollow, tainted with the bitter taste of regret. He had played the game, and won. But at what cost? The question echoed in the silent chambers of his mind, a symphony of unresolved notes. He looked out the window once more—the city sprawling, chaotic, but now carrying an entirely new and unsettling meaning. The long shadow of Sharon Cohen—and his own involvement in his capture—stretched far beyond the case file, reaching into the very core of his being. The darkness he had fought against now resided within him, a chilling reminder of the moral complexities of justice. The pursuit of truth, he now understood, often left a trail of moral ambiguity and self-doubt in its wake. The hunt was over, but the reckoning had only just begun—a war waged not against a criminal, but against the very fabric of his own conscience.

Miriams Recovery

The sterile scent of antiseptic lingered in the air, a sharp contrast to the vibrant life Miriam had once known. The hospital room, though comfortable, felt more like a cage, its walls slowly closing in on her with each passing hour. The bruises, both physical and emotional, were fading, but the memories remained—vivid, unforgiving. Sharon's betrayal, the violence, the chilling violation of trust—these were wounds that wouldn't heal easily. She traced the faint scar on her arm, a physical mark of the deeper emotional scars within.

Tommy's presence had been a lifeline, a beacon in the darkness. His quiet strength and unwavering support gave her the courage to confront the demons that haunted her. He didn't press for details, didn't push her to recount the horrors she'd endured. Instead, he simply was—a solid, reassuring presence. His hand in hers, offering silent comfort. He'd sit by her bedside for hours, reading aloud from a worn copy of Hemingway, his voice a soothing balm to her fractured spirit. His presence was sanctuary, a refuge from the storm within.

But even Tommy's steadfast support couldn't fully erase the shadow of Sharon's actions. The betrayal was a deep wound, a crack in her foundation. She had trusted him implicitly, had shared her life, her dreams, her vulnerabilities with him. To have that trust shattered so brutally, so violently, had shaken her to her core. The man she thought she knew, the man she had loved, had turned out to be a monster—a ruthless predator disguised in a lover's guise. The realization was a bitter pill, leaving a nauseating taste of disillusionment and despair.

The therapy sessions were slow and agonizing. Dr. Anya Sharma, a renowned trauma specialist, guided Miriam patiently through the labyrinth of her pain. The sessions were fraught with emotion—tears, anger, and moments of intense frustration. Miriam relived the trauma, piece by agonizing piece, under Dr. Sharma's watchful eye. Each session was a small victory, a step forward in her long, arduous journey toward healing. She learned to confront her fears, to acknowledge her pain, and to accept that what had happened was not her fault.

One session focused on the manipulative tactics Sharon had used to gain her trust. Dr. Sharma helped Miriam recognize the subtle ways he had controlled her, eroded her self-esteem, and ultimately isolated her from her support system. It was painful, but necessary. Understanding the mechanisms of his manipulation empowered Miriam, giving her the strength to reclaim her autonomy.

Another session centered on forgiveness—not forgiveness of Sharon—that would take time, perhaps a lifetime—but forgiveness of herself. Miriam had been harsh on herself, blaming herself for being vulnerable, for trusting someone who ultimately betrayed her. Dr. Sharma helped her see that vulnerability wasn't weakness; being open to love was a strength, and Sharon's actions reflected his own flaws, not hers.

The physical recovery had been swift, but the emotional scars lingered. Nightmares plagued Miriam—vivid, terrifying replays of the violence she had endured. She'd wake up screaming, drenched in sweat, her heart pounding. Tommy would always be there, comforting her, holding her close until the fear subsided. He'd speak softly, his voice a calming presence—a reminder that she was safe, that she was loved.

Miriam also found solace in the support of friends and family. They rallied around her, offering love and strength, helping her navigate the treacherous waters of her recovery. Their presence was a lifeline, a reminder that she wasn't alone, that she was surrounded by people who cared deeply for her. They were her anchors, keeping her grounded amid the storm.

The police investigation had faded into the background, a chapter closed but not forgotten. Sharon Cohen's arrest brought a sense of closure, but it didn't erase the trauma. It was a step toward justice, but justice couldn't undo the damage—it couldn't erase the memories or the pain.

One day, while browsing through old photos, Miriam stumbled upon a picture of herself and Sharon, taken during happier times. A wave of sadness washed over her, a bittersweet reminder of the life that had been stolen. But this time, the sadness was not crippling. It was a feeling she could acknowledge, process, and accept as part of her journey. She gently placed the photo back in the album, quietly acknowledging a past that could no longer define her.

As the days turned into weeks, and the weeks into months, Miriam began to reclaim her life. She returned to work slowly, cautiously. The transition wasn't easy, but her colleagues were supportive and patient. She learned to manage her anxiety, to cope with the lingering effects of trauma.

Miriam began painting again, an old hobby she had abandoned during the darkest days of her ordeal. The canvas became a safe space, a way to express emotions she couldn't put into words. The vibrant colors and flowing lines became a testament to her resilience—a symbol of her journey from darkness into light.

Her relationship with Tommy deepened. They had navigated a difficult path together, one forged in the crucible of shared trauma and mutual support. Their bond, tested and strengthened by adversity, emerged stronger and more profound than ever before. He didn't replace Sharon—he became something entirely different: a source of genuine love and unconditional support, a safe harbor in the storm.

The long shadow of Sharon Cohen still lingered, but it no longer dominated her life. It was part of her story—a reminder of the darkness she had survived—but it no longer held her captive. Miriam had found her strength, her voice, her path to healing. She was a survivor, and her journey was a testament to the remarkable resilience of the human spirit, to hope, and to love. The scars remained, both visible and invisible, but they were markers of her strength, a map of her journey—a reminder of battles fought and a life reclaimed. The future remained uncertain, but for the first time in a long while, Miriam felt ready to face it, to embrace it, to build a life worthy of the battles she had fought and the strength she had discovered within herself. Healing was ongoing—a continuous process of self-discovery and acceptance—but she was finally on the path to a future where the darkness was no longer a dominant force, but a fading shadow in the landscape of her life. The long journey to healing was far from over, but Miriam, with Tommy by her side, was walking toward the light.

Unresolved Questions

The rhythmic tick-tock of the clock on the wall seemed to mock the stillness of the interrogation room. Detective Pickens sat across from the subdued figure of Cohen, the notorious Mossad renegade. The air was thick with unspoken tension, a palpable silence weighed down by the heavy burden of unanswered questions. Though the successful apprehension marked the culmination of a painstaking investigation, aided by a stroke of luck with the wiretap on Miriam's phone, it felt anticlimactic. The capture itself had been a mere formality; the true battle now lay in unraveling the intricate web of Cohen's past—a labyrinth of betrayals, double-crosses, and violence that spanned continents and reached into the highest echelons of power.

Despite his success, Pickens felt a profound sense of unease. Cohen's arrest hadn't brought closure; instead, it had opened Pandora's Box, flooding him with unresolved issues. The meticulous planning behind the Al-Qaeda bombing plot, the enigmatic role of the Israeli government in the seemingly coincidental removal of gold reserves from the World Trade Center before the attack—these lingering questions gnawed at him. The complex interactions between Cohen, the Israeli intelligence agency, and the shadowy underworld of international organized crime were far from fully understood. The trail of bodies, the pattern of meticulously planned heists targeting wealthy Israelis and seemingly random Pakistani cab drivers, and the final contract to eliminate a Muslim Brotherhood infiltrator in the US government—each piece pointed to a much larger, more sinister conspiracy.

But perhaps the most perplexing aspect was the sheer audacity of Cohen's actions. His betrayal of Mossad, his plunge into a life of crime, his violent assault on Miriam—these were not the actions of a man acting under duress or coercion. They were calculated moves, suggesting a deliberate unraveling of his own life—a self-destructive path that seemed almost intentional. Was it a desperate cry for attention? A calculated attempt to expose a greater conspiracy? Or was it the tragic unraveling of a deeply troubled, damaged individual?

Pickens knew Cohen wouldn't easily give up his secrets. He was a master manipulator, skilled in the art of deception. Years spent honing his craft in the shadows had taught him how to play both sides against each other, building a reputation for ruthlessness and unpredictability. Cohen wouldn't crack under pressure. He would likely use the interrogation to manipulate Pickens, sowing discord and possibly sending a final, cryptic message. The silence between them was punctuated only by the distant sirens of the city, their mournful symphony echoing the complexity of the case.

The interrogation began slowly, a delicate dance of carefully chosen words and calculated silences. Pickens, armed with a mountain of evidence, began by meticulously laying out Cohen's criminal activities, presenting him with irrefutable proof. He hoped to overwhelm him with the sheer weight of his crimes. But Cohen remained unmoved, his eyes betraying nothing but cold, calculating intelligence. His answers were clipped, evasive, and practiced—his gaze unyielding. He acknowledged his actions but refused to elaborate, offering only carefully constructed narratives that lacked real emotion or remorse.

Pickens shifted his approach. He tried appealing to Cohen's sense of patriotism, suggesting that his actions had jeopardized Israeli national security. He brought up the possible connections to the bombing, hinting at a larger cover-up. But Cohen merely scoffed, a sardonic smile playing on his lips. He seemed almost amused by Pickens' efforts.

He dismissed any accusations of betraying his country, claiming that it was the government that had betrayed him. His disillusionment, he insisted, stemmed from their cynical manipulation and ruthless disregard for human life.

The hours stretched into a grueling marathon of interrogation, a game of cat and mouse in which Cohen clearly held the upper hand. He was a master storyteller, weaving intricate tales that obscured the truth, shifting the narrative to suit his purposes. With his knowledge of intelligence operations, he challenged Pickens' assumptions, questioning the validity of the evidence and exploiting every loophole in the legal process. It was clear he reveled in the intellectual duel—the challenge of outwitting his adversary.

Pickens felt his frustration mounting. He knew Cohen was withholding information, but extracting it proved to be an impossible task. He changed tactics again, attempting to connect with Cohen on a personal level by broaching the subject of Miriam. He spoke of her resilience, her strength, her determination to rebuild her life. He hoped that a flicker of remorse, even a trace of guilt, might crack Cohen's hardened exterior.

But Cohen remained impervious. He spoke of Miriam with detached indifference, reducing her to nothing more than a pawn in a larger game—a woman he had used and discarded. His words were devoid of emotion, a chilling testament to his callousness.

The mention of Miriam, rather than provoking remorse, seemed only to fuel his amusement. It became evident that his past was a carefully constructed narrative, designed to manipulate and control. He spoke of his life, but what he painted was not reality—it was a selective fiction, a carefully curated version of events meant to obscure more than reveal.

As the interrogation drew to a close, Pickens realized he was losing the battle. Cohen was not merely a criminal; he was a ghost, a shadowy figure who existed in the gray area between intelligence operations and organized crime. He was a master of deception, adept at manipulating the system and leaving a trail of ambiguities and unanswered questions in his wake. Cohen would likely remain a mystery until his last breath, leaving authorities to piece together a puzzle with many missing pieces. The only certainty was that Cohen's case was not just a criminal investigation; it was a complex geopolitical thriller—a twisted tale of betrayal, ambition, and the dark underbelly of international politics.

The long shadow of Sharon Cohen, far from receding, stretched further into the darkness, leaving countless questions unanswered—a chilling reminder of the murky world he inhabited, a world where truth and deception danced a perilous tango, leaving lasting consequences and unanswered questions in its wake.

The unanswered questions hung heavy in the air long after Cohen was transferred to a maximum-security facility. The precise nature of his involvement in the Al-Qaeda plot, the extent of the Israeli government's complicity, and the true purpose behind his criminal activities—all remained shrouded in mystery. Pickens, weary but resolute, knew that the investigation was far from over. It had opened a door to a world of hidden agendas and dark secrets—a world that would require years of investigation to fully uncover. The pursuit of truth, he realized, was an unending process, a relentless search for answers in a world where lies often wore the mask of truth and shadows concealed secrets darker than the imagination could fathom. The case of Sharon Cohen was not closed; it was merely suspended, awaiting further developments. A chilling testament to the complexities of the human heart and the seductive nature of power, the story was far from finished, and the shadows held secrets yet to be revealed—secrets woven into a puzzle of intrigue and deception that stretched across continents and into the heart of global politics.

The Aftermath

The transfer to the maximum-security facility unfolded like a blur of harsh fluorescent lights, echoing metallic clanks, and the unmistakable, sterile scent of disinfectant. Despite his defiance during the arrest, Cohen felt an unexpected sensation—relief? The adrenaline that had once fueled his reckless existence was now fading, replaced by an overwhelming exhaustion. The game, it seemed, had come to an end. But the consequences, Cohen knew, were only beginning.

For Miriam, the aftermath was a slow, agonizing unraveling. The wiretap on her phone, initially intended to ensnare Cohen, had exposed her own compromised position. Her involvement with him—once a desperate attempt to reclaim a shard of her lost past—had left her vulnerable, now under the scrutiny of both Mossad and the NYPD. No longer the elusive operative moving in the shadows, Miriam had become a pawn in a far larger game. Her life now lay bare, exposed to public attention, and the investigation into her activities had devolved into a maze of half-truths and evasions. Though Mossad initially seethed with outrage at Cohen's betrayal, they were far more focused on protecting their interests than seeking her justice. They needed her silence, a silence bought with a promise of immunity, a gilded cage disguised as freedom. Miriam found herself adrift in an ocean of uncertainty, haunted by the ghost of Cohen's brutality and the knowledge of her own complicity.

Detective Pickens, despite the seeming closure of Cohen's case, found himself entangled by the long shadows it cast. The relentless pursuit of truth consumed him. Cohen's connections to the Israeli government, and the casually mentioned removal of gold reserves from the World Trade Center before the Al-

Qaeda bombing—these threads tugged at Pickens' conscience. He knew that chasing them could be dangerous, perhaps even suicidal, but he couldn't turn away. The official narrative swept these details aside, branding them as inconsequential, but to Pickens, they were beacons leading deeper into a world of international intrigue. His obsession with uncovering the truth began to alienate him from his colleagues, casting him as a solitary figure in pursuit of elusive shadows.

The fallout reached far beyond the immediate players. The Muslim Brotherhood's internal struggle, the very catalyst for Cohen's final contract, raged on. The assassination attempt aimed at infiltrating the U.S. government had failed, but it only intensified the internal conflict within the organization. The failed operation revealed deep divisions, accelerating a schism that shattered the Brotherhood from within. The ripple effect cascaded throughout the global jihadist movement, as competing factions vied for power in the resulting vacuum. The operation's objectives and the identity of the infiltrator, however, remained shrouded in mystery. This lingering question fueled suspicion and unrest within intelligence agencies around the world.

Within the Israeli mob in Morocco, Cohen's absence ignited a power vacuum, triggering a brutal internal war for dominance. The uneasy truce maintained by Cohen's iron fist dissolved into bloody conflict, marked by ambushes, assassinations, and escalating violence. His former associates, now desperate to secure their own positions, resorted to ruthless tactics to consolidate power. The drug trade, once a tightly controlled operation under Cohen's reign, spiraled into chaos, further destabilizing an already fragile region. His absence had disrupted a delicate balance maintained through calculated cruelty and fear, leaving a profound, dangerous vacuum.

Meanwhile, the Israeli government—despite its outward indifference—felt the weight of Cohen's actions. Though no explicit evidence had emerged, the implications of their possible complicity in the Al-Qaeda bombing cast a long, ominous shadow over their international standing. Ongoing investigations by various international bodies heightened the pressure, threatening political instability. The whispers of Israel's manipulation of global events for its own political and economic gain swirled, and the specter of international sanctions loomed large.

The reverberations of Cohen's actions extended far beyond immediate consequences. The Al-Qaeda bombing, which Cohen had once sought to prevent, left a chilling mark on the international landscape, reminding everyone that global terrorism was an ever-present threat. Ironically, Cohen's actions, though initially motivated by a desire to prevent catastrophe, had inadvertently shifted global power dynamics. They had contributed to an atmosphere of instability and mistrust between nations. His betrayal of Mossad had eroded public confidence in Israeli intelligence agencies, even as it emboldened global terrorist organizations, revealing the unintended consequences of covert operations and the unpredictable nature of geopolitics.

The story of Sharon Cohen stands as a stark reminder of espionage's human cost, the moral ambiguities inherent in international intrigue, and the often-unforeseen consequences of actions taken in the name of national security. His fall from grace—from revered agent to notorious criminal—was a testament to the seductive allure of power and the corrosive nature of unchecked ambition. His legacy continued to resonate, echoing across continents, exposing the fragility of global security and the enduring power of secrets.

Even in incarceration, his story remained a haunting testament to betrayal, violence, and political machinations, a chilling reflection of the darkness beneath international relations. Investigations continued, shadows deepened, and the pursuit of truth—relentless and perhaps unattainable—carried on. The silence in the maximum-security facility was broken only by the rhythmic tick-tock of a clock, a grim counterpoint to the ongoing unraveling of consequences that stretched far beyond the confines of any prison cell.

The Legacy of Deception

The rhythmic clang of the steel door as it slid shut behind him marked the final, definitive punctuation of a life lived on the razor's edge. The fleeting relief he had once felt during his arrest was now a distant memory, replaced by a gnawing unease that burrowed deep into his bones. He wasn't merely incarcerated; he had become a symbol— a cautionary tale whispered in hushed tones in the shadowy corners of the intelligence world and the murky backrooms of organized crime. With chilling clarity, he realized his legacy was one of deception.

The deception had started subtly, a gradual erosion of his ideals. The initial mission—the one involving the Al-Qaeda plot and the suspiciously convenient removal of Israeli gold reserves from the World Trade Center—had been presented as a noble endeavor, a preemptive strike against a catastrophic threat. Yet, the deeper he delved, the more he questioned the official narrative. The blatant disregard for collateral damage, the convenient scapegoating, the complete lack of acknowledgment for his role in averting a global catastrophe— it all chipped away at his faith in the very system he had sworn to uphold.

Disillusionment bred bitterness, a festering resentment that poisoned his soul. The betrayal he felt from Mossad wasn't simply about the lack of recognition; it was a profound violation of trust, a betrayal of the unspoken contract between agent and agency. This betrayal fueled his descent into the criminal underworld, a descent that was as much an escape from his past as a reckless embrace of a nihilistic present. He traded the sophisticated tools of espionage for the brutal instruments of the underworld, his meticulously honed skills now employed in acts of violence and theft. The line between right and wrong blurred, then vanished entirely, consumed by the intoxicating haze of power and impunity.

Each act of deception, each betrayal, built upon the last, creating a pyramid of lies that threatened to crush him under its weight. His relationship with Miriam, once a source of comfort and strength, became yet another casualty of his twisted morality. The violence he inflicted upon her— a brutal act of control born from his own inner turmoil— shattered the remnants of his former self. He became a ghost, a phantom drifting through the shadows, his actions leaving a trail of destruction in their wake. The murders, the robberies, the contract to eliminate the Muslim Brotherhood operative— all were pieces of the same fractured puzzle, each act a testament to his spiraling descent.

The repercussions of his actions rippled far beyond his own personal downfall. His betrayal of Mossad had jeopardized countless operations, compromised intelligence networks, and left gaping holes in the fabric of national security. The aftershocks were devastating, shaking governments and alliances to their core. His criminal activities had destabilized several organizations, sparking turf wars and violent conflicts. Innocent lives were lost, families shattered, all because of the long shadow cast by his deceit. The seemingly isolated acts of violence were, in reality, interconnected threads in a complex web of intrigue and betrayal, highlighting the dangerous interconnectedness of global politics and organized crime.

Detective Tommy Pickens, unwittingly caught in the crosshairs of Cohen's chaotic legacy, became a symbol of the innocent swept up in the undertow of his actions. Initially focused on seemingly unrelated crimes, Pickens's investigation slowly uncovered the sinister network of corruption and violence orchestrated by Cohen. His relationship with Miriam, Cohen's former girlfriend, thrust him into the eye of the storm, making him a prime target for Cohen's wrath. Pickens's dogged pursuit of justice transformed into a personal crusade, a relentless attempt to expose Cohen's web of deception and bring him to account.

The wiretap on Miriam's phone, a seemingly insignificant piece of technology, became the keystone that brought Cohen's elaborate house of cards crashing down. It was the final act of betrayal, an almost cosmic-scale violation of trust. He had underestimated the power of technology, the reach of law enforcement, and the unwavering resolve of a determined detective. The arrest and subsequent transfer to the maximum-security facility— these were not just endings, but the beginning of a much longer and more complex journey. His incarceration didn't erase his legacy; it only cemented it.

But his legacy wasn't solely defined by violence and betrayal. Cohen's story also served as a stark testament to humanity's capacity for self-destruction, a chilling exploration of the psychological toll of living a life built on lies and deceit. The consequences of his actions were far-reaching, affecting not only his personal life but also the geopolitical landscape. He became a cautionary tale, a reminder of the precarious balance between power and responsibility, the ethical quagmire inherent in the world of espionage, and the devastating effects of unchecked ambition.

Even within the confines of his prison cell, the long shadow of his deception stretched across continents. Investigations continued, unraveling further layers of the web of lies he had spun. The trials unfolded, revealing the full extent of his crimes, the names of his accomplices, and the depth of the corruption. His testimony— whether forced or voluntary— provided a chilling insight into the inner workings of both the intelligence community and the criminal underworld, exposing the collusion, betrayals, and systemic flaws that allowed individuals like him to thrive.

His story became a grim reminder of how easily the lines blur between national security and criminal enterprise. The ethical boundaries he so conveniently crossed allowed him to exploit situations for personal gain, demonstrating how those tasked with protecting national security could so easily become corrupted. The moral ambiguities of his actions— initially justified by the greater good, but quickly devolving into a chaotic pursuit of self-aggrandizement— left an indelible mark on all who encountered his tale, lingering with a sense of unease and moral ambiguity.

The repercussions of Cohen's actions extended far beyond the immediate. His betrayal caused a seismic shift in global trust, rattling alliances and exposing vulnerabilities in security networks. The implications spread beyond governments, extending to multinational corporations and transnational organizations, raising concerns about the security of international commerce and sensitive information. His case became a subject of academic analysis, prompting sweeping reforms in intelligence gathering and counterterrorism strategies.

The silence of his cell, once a symbol of isolation, now echoed with the weight of his choices. The rhythmic tick-tock of a clock became the soundtrack to his unraveling life, the ticking away of the time he had left to reflect on the consequences of his decisions. The long shadow of Sharon Cohen— the man, the agent, the criminal— would continue to cast its dark pall over the world long after his incarceration, a chilling testament to the lasting power of deception and the human capacity for both great good and unfathomable evil. His story, a cautionary tale wrapped in intrigue, serves as a stark reminder that even in the shadows, the price of deception is always paid— and often, the cost is far greater than anyone could anticipate.

Cohens Reflection

The cold, damp stone pressed against my cheek, a familiar discomfort in this concrete coffin. The rhythmic clang of a distant cell door echoed the monotonous beat of my own heart, a drum solo of regret playing out in the vast silence of my confinement. They called it a maximum-security prison, but it felt more like a mausoleum—a tomb for the remnants of a life I'd once considered thrilling. Now, it was just a slow, agonizing decay.

Ten years. Ten years since the Moroccan sun beat down on my skin, ten years since adrenaline coursed through my veins during high-stakes chases and deadly encounters. Ten years since I tasted the bitter tang of betrayal, the metallic scent of blood, and the chilling emptiness of a life devoid of any genuine connection. Ten years since Miriam's terrified eyes burned into my memory, a constant reminder of the monstrous choices I had made.

It had all started with a noble cause, or at least that's what they told me. Operation Nightingale. Infiltrating Al-Qaeda, preventing a catastrophic attack—a patriotic duty, they claimed. But the truth was far more cynical. The gold—the gold that vanished from the World Trade Center right under the noses of the world's intelligence agencies—that was the real story. A desperate, cynical play for power by a government that cared little for its operatives, only for its own self-preservation. My actions, my sacrifices, were simply pawns in a much larger game, a game I was now paying the ultimate price for.

Mossad had used me, discarded me like a broken tool. And the Israeli mob, those vultures, had simply taken advantage of my brokenness. I thought I was playing them, using their connections to build my own power. I was a fool. They were just as ruthless, just as treacherous as Mossad, perhaps more so. There was no loyalty, no honor among thieves—a lesson I learned the hard way, etched into my soul with every betrayal and every violent act.

Miriam. The thought of her still sent a jolt of icy fear through me, mingled with a sickening wave of remorse. She was everything I wasn't: honest, compassionate, fiercely loyal. And I had repaid her trust with violence—a brutal act that shattered not only her body but also the fragile hope I had once harbored for something real. Her face, etched with pain and betrayal, haunts my dreams, a constant reminder of the monster I had become.

Pickens. That relentless NYPD detective, driven by righteous anger and fueled by his relationship with Miriam. He was my nemesis, the embodiment of the justice I had so brutally evaded for so long. He'd followed my trail of destruction, piecing together the puzzle of my crimes, one body, one betrayal at a time. He saw through the layers of deception, the carefully constructed façade I'd erected to hide my shame and guilt. He saw the darkness in me—the darkness I had embraced so readily.

The Muslim Brotherhood contract... that was the pinnacle of my depravity. A cold, calculated decision driven by greed and a desperate need for validation. Eliminating a potential threat to the US government—for a price. It was a hollow victory, a testament to my moral bankruptcy. I had become the very thing I had sworn to fight against—a weapon for hire, a mercenary without a conscience.

The prison walls seemed to close in, the silence amplifying the cacophony of my memories. Each day was a repetition of the last, a bleak cycle of regret and self-loathing. I'd tried to find some solace in the monotonous routine, in the simple act of survival, but the ghosts of my past wouldn't let me rest. They clung to me like shadows, relentless and unforgiving.

The irony wasn't lost on me. I, Sharon Cohen, the ghost who haunted the corridors of power, now haunted by the ghosts of my own making. The master manipulator, outsmarted and confined. The ruthless operative, reduced to a broken, defeated man. The sophisticated spy, stripped bare, exposed for the hollow shell I had become.

They say time heals all wounds. But some wounds, some scars, run too deep. The scars on my soul are etched in indelible ink, reminders of the choices I made, the lives I destroyed. There's no redemption here, no chance for a clean slate. Only the bitter taste of consequences, the weight of my sins pressing down on me, heavier than these cold, unforgiving walls.

The silence of the cell is broken only by the rasp of my breath, the echo of my own heartbeat, the relentless ticking of a clock that counts down to an uncertain future. A future where the sands of time continue to slip through my fingers, each grain representing a moment I can never reclaim, a moment I can never undo. A future where the price of my betrayals will be paid in full, a debt I can never repay.

I think of Miriam sometimes, wondering if she ever found peace, if she ever forgave me. The thought is a small flicker of hope in the vast emptiness, a fleeting moment of light in the suffocating darkness. Maybe, just maybe, somewhere in the quiet corners of her heart, there's a trace of forgiveness. A sliver of understanding. But that is just a wish, a faint hope in the desolate landscape of my soul.

Pickens... I wonder if he ever truly understood the depth of my corruption, the web of lies I'd spun. He saw the surface—the acts of violence, the betrayals. But did he see the disillusionment, the pain, the crushing weight of betrayal that drove me to such extremes? Probably not. Justice, it seems, is a blunt instrument, incapable of dissecting the complexities of the human heart, incapable of understanding the subtleties of motivation.

The truth is, I don't expect forgiveness. I don't deserve it. My actions have spoken for themselves, leaving an indelible mark on the lives of those I've touched. The damage is done, irreversible. All that remains is to accept the consequences, to endure the slow, agonizing process of reckoning with the choices I've made. To face the truth, however brutal, however unforgiving.

The sands of time continue to fall, each grain a testament to the passage of time, a relentless march toward an unknown end. But even as the sands slip through my fingers, one thing remains constant: the unwavering, unrelenting weight of guilt. The heavy, inescapable burden of knowing that the price of my ambition was far, far higher than I ever could have imagined. The chilling realization that some actions cast shadows that stretch across a lifetime, across generations, leaving an echo of darkness that never truly fades. The sands of time may bury the past, but they cannot erase the memories, the regrets, the indelible stain of my betrayal. And in the suffocating silence of this cell, that's all that matters. That's all that remains.

Pickenss Conclusion

The metallic tang of blood still lingered in the air, a phantom scent that clung long after the cleanup crew had scrubbed the interrogation room. Even the antiseptic couldn't erase the memory of Cohen's defiance—the chilling glint in his eyes as he spat out his last confession, a confession that felt less like a confession and more like a boast. He painted a portrait of himself as a predator, a master manipulator, a creature born of shadows and thriving in darkness. And, in a twisted way, I had to admit, he was all of those things—and more.

Cohen's arrest felt like the final punctuation in a sprawling, chaotic sentence. The sentence that had been my life for the past year—a relentless pursuit through the labyrinthine alleys of organized crime and the treacherous terrain of international espionage. It had started with a string of seemingly random murders—wealthy Israelis, Pakistani cab drivers—victims who appeared unconnected, save for a chilling thread that bound them: Sharon Cohen. The seemingly insignificant details—a specific type of knife, a signature method of disposing of the bodies, a particular brand of cigarette found at each scene—had, like fragments of a shattered mirror, slowly reflected back a terrifying truth.

But the truth wasn't just about the murders. It was about the intricate web of deceit, the layers of lies Cohen had spun—a web so tightly woven it nearly ensnared me. It had been Miriam, Cohen's ex-girlfriend, who had provided the initial break in the case. Her testimony, fraught with fear and reluctant betrayal, painted a picture of a man capable of unimaginable cruelty, a man willing to sacrifice anything—and anyone—in his relentless pursuit of power and profit. Her vulnerability had become a tool in my investigation, her past intertwined with Cohen's becoming the key to unlocking the truth. And yet, I couldn't shake the feeling that I had barely scratched the surface.

There were still unanswered questions—gaps in the narrative, shadows lurking at the periphery. The Al-Qaeda plot, the Israeli government's preemptive removal of gold reserves from the World Trade Center, the Israeli mob's involvement in Morocco—these were all pieces of a larger puzzle, a puzzle so complex it threatened to overwhelm even my seasoned investigative skills. The connections were tenuous, shadowy, hinting at a world far beyond the reach of the law—a world where nations danced a deadly tango, and where the lines between friend and foe, loyalty and betrayal, blurred into indistinguishable shades of grey.

Cohen's case had exposed a gaping wound in the fabric of international security. It revealed the ease with which individuals could manipulate power, exploit vulnerabilities, and orchestrate chaos on a global scale. It showed how even the most meticulously crafted plans could unravel, how alliances could shift in an instant, and how the very foundations of trust could crumble beneath the weight of ambition and greed. I thought of the countless lives touched by Cohen's actions—the families torn apart, the communities shattered, the trust betrayed. It was a heavy burden to bear, the knowledge that one man could inflict such widespread damage.

The trial was a whirlwind of legal maneuvering, tense courtroom confrontations, and the chilling revelation of Cohen's ruthless efficiency. His testimony was a performance—calculated indifference at its finest. He offered no remorse, no apologies, only cold, calculating acceptance of his fate. A master manipulator, even in defeat, he used the legal system as yet another tool to assert his control, maintaining a semblance of power, even from behind bars.

But the prosecution's case, bolstered by Miriam's testimony and mountains of evidence, was overwhelming. The jury's verdict came swiftly—a unanimous guilty plea. The sentence—life imprisonment without parole—felt like a fitting conclusion, though a cold, insufficient recompense for the damage he had wrought. But the case left its mark on me, an indelible scar.

The nights following the trial were restless, haunted by the faces of Cohen's victims, by the weight of the untold stories buried beneath the surface. I saw the fear in Miriam's eyes, the trauma etched into her face—a constant reminder of the human cost of Cohen's actions. I started seeing Cohen's ghost in the shadows of the city, his malevolent presence hanging in the air, a chilling echo of the chaos he had unleashed. The city that never sleeps felt suffocating, its constant noise and activity a mocking reminder of the pervasive silence that had settled over the lives of his victims.

The city was different now—the shadows seemed deeper, the faces more suspect. The experience had changed me, stripping away some of my naiveté, replacing it with a hard-won cynicism. I now looked beyond the surface, questioning everything, scrutinizing each interaction for hidden motives and unspoken truths. The city's glittering façade had been shattered, revealing the dark underbelly I had only glimpsed before. The case had irrevocably altered my perception of good and evil, of justice and revenge.

My relationship with Miriam, forged in the crucible of the investigation, evolved into something deeper—a connection built on shared trauma and mutual understanding. She was a survivor, a woman who had faced unimaginable horrors and emerged with her spirit unbroken. Her strength, her resilience, became a constant source of inspiration. Our bond, formed through Cohen's crimes, transcended mere companionship. We were survivors, bound by a shared understanding of the darkness that lurked beneath the surface of the world. Yet, the shared trauma cast a long shadow. The fear lingered—a silent presence in our lives. The knowledge that Cohen's reach extended far beyond the confines of his cell cast a chilling pall over our future. He may have been behind bars, but the echoes of his actions still resonated.

The case had taken its toll. The long hours, the relentless pressure, the emotional intensity—it had worn me down, leaving me emotionally drained, spiritually depleted. I found myself questioning the nature of my work, the purpose of my relentless pursuit of justice. I started seeing the city through the eyes of a man wounded by his experiences. My perspective had changed forever. I was a detective, yes, but I was also a man carrying the weight of the world on his shoulders.

But perhaps that's what makes us detectives—the drive to pursue justice, even when the darkness threatens to consume us. The relentless pursuit of truth, the unwavering commitment to justice, despite the risks, despite the personal cost—this is what keeps us going. This is what compels us to confront the darkness and expose the lies. We are guardians of the city, protectors of the innocent, even if the price of our vigilance is our own peace of mind.

The sands of time continued to fall, but now, I realized, they were not only symbols of the passage of time, but reminders of the legacy we leave behind. Cohen's legacy was one of violence and destruction. Mine, I hoped, would be one of justice. The fight against the darkness was far from over, but I would continue, driven by a renewed sense of purpose, strengthened by the scars of experience. The city, with all its shadows and secrets, was still my domain. And I would continue to patrol its streets—vigilant, relentless, always on the lookout for the next predator, the next storm gathering on the horizon. The game was far from over. The sands of time may bury the past, but the fight continues. The weight of the city, its dark secrets, and its relentless pursuit of justice would remain.

Miriams New Beginning

The scent of jasmine and sea salt hung heavily in the air, a stark contrast to the metallic tang of blood that had haunted Miriam for months. She sat on the balcony of her small apartment overlooking the Mediterranean, a fragile cup of mint tea warming her hands. The sun, a molten orb sinking toward the horizon, painted the sky in hues of fiery orange and soft lavender. It was a breathtaking view, a beautiful backdrop to a life she was painstakingly rebuilding, brick by agonizing brick.

Leaving New York had been a necessity, a desperate flight from the ghosts of Sharon Cohen and the chilling echo of his violence. She had severed ties, not just with him, but with the life that had ensnared her. The NYPD, initially sympathetic, had eventually grown wary of her evasiveness, their questions probing deeper than she was willing to allow. The details of her involvement with Cohen—the clandestine operations, the betrayals—remained a tightly sealed compartment in her mind, a Pandora's Box she dared not open. She had left behind the life of a spy, the adrenaline, the danger, the constant fear. She had traded it for anonymity, for a quiet existence where the only shadows were those cast by the setting sun.

This small coastal town in southern Spain felt a million miles away from the harsh realities of her past. The pace of life was slower, gentler. The locals, initially hesitant, had slowly warmed to her, drawn in by her quiet demeanor and the unspoken sorrow lingering in her eyes. She found solace in the simple rhythms of daily life—the early morning market bustling with energy, the aroma of fresh bread wafting from the nearby bakery, the rhythmic crash of waves against the shore. She took long walks along the beach, the sand cool and soothing beneath her feet, the vast expanse of the sea a symbol of the boundless potential for healing.

She started small, taking a part-time job at a local bookstore, surrounded by the comforting scent of old paper and ink. The job was far removed from the high-stakes world she'd once inhabited, but it offered a sense of normalcy, a routine to anchor her days. The customers, mostly tourists and retirees, were kind and unassuming, offering her small, quiet conversations that were a welcome respite from the inner turmoil that still gnawed at her. She found herself drawn to poetry, its lyrical cadence a balm to her wounded soul. She devoured books, finding solace in fictional worlds far removed from her own troubled reality.

The healing process wasn't linear. There were days when the nightmares returned—vivid and relentless, dragging her back to the chilling darkness of Cohen's violence. The memories, sharp and unforgiving, pierced through the fragile peace she had painstakingly constructed. On those days, she would find herself staring out at the sea, the vastness of the ocean mirroring the immensity of her grief. The salty air, however, carried a certain cleansing power; the rhythmic sound of the waves helped to wash away the residue of her pain.

She sought out a therapist, a kind woman with gentle hands and wise eyes. The sessions were excruciating at first, forcing her to confront the trauma she had buried deep within. Slowly, tentatively, she began to peel back the layers of her pain, revealing the scars of betrayal and the wounds of abandonment. The therapist helped her understand that healing was a journey, not a destination, a process of self-discovery that would take time and unwavering commitment.

She encouraged Miriam to embrace the present, to find beauty in the everyday, to rediscover her own strength and resilience.

Miriam started painting again, a passion she had abandoned years ago in the relentless pursuit of her espionage career. Her canvases became a canvas for her emotions, a way to express the turmoil within. The colors, vibrant and bold, reflected the spectrum of her feelings—the darkness of her past, the fragility of her present, and the tentative hope for the future. She began exhibiting her work at local art galleries, hesitant at first, then emboldened by the positive responses she received. Her art became a form of therapy, a way to communicate without words, to share her pain and resilience with the world.

Her relationship with Tommy Pickens remained a complex, unspoken chapter. They hadn't spoken since she'd fled New York, their last conversation a cacophony of accusations and unspoken grief. She knew he was still investigating Cohen's activities, that he was haunted by the same darkness that had consumed her. She felt a pang of guilt, a responsibility to reach out, to offer him some solace. But the fear, the ingrained instinct to protect herself, held her back.

One evening, she received an unexpected email from him. It was brief, simply stating his intention to visit her in Spain. The message brought a wave of anxiety but also a flicker of hope. She realized that running away had only served to delay the inevitable confrontation with her past. She owed it to herself, to Tommy, to face the truth, however painful it might be. His arrival would be a catalyst, a turning point in her journey toward healing. It would be a test, a challenge, but she was ready to face it, armed with the strength she had painstakingly reclaimed. The sands of time, once a symbol of her despair, now felt like a measure of her enduring spirit, a testament to her resilience. She was not a victim; she was a survivor. And she was ready to finally begin living again.

The sun dipped below the horizon, casting long shadows across her balcony, but the darkness no longer held the same power. A new dawn was breaking, and Miriam was ready to greet it.

The Unfinished Game

The Spanish sun beat down on Sharon Cohen as he stepped off the plane in Málaga. He hadn't shaved in days, his usually meticulous appearance now a disheveled mess, mirroring the inner turmoil that churned within him. The email, a simple and almost apologetic note, had been a gamble. He'd hoped, perhaps foolishly, for some semblance of closure, a chance to explain, to atone—though deep down, he knew atonement was not something he truly deserved. He had seen Miriam's fear in the surveillance footage, the raw terror in her eyes as he'd dragged her into the car, the brutal efficiency with which he'd silenced her scream. That image, forever etched into the darkest corners of his mind, was a constant, gnawing reminder of the monster he had become.

Months spent in a Moroccan prison—a squalid hole where the stench of desperation clung to the air like a second skin—had not broken him physically, but emotionally. The gnawing emptiness, the realization that his carefully constructed life, built on lies and betrayals, had crumbled to dust, had shattered him in ways he couldn't have anticipated. He'd lost everything: his career, his freedom, his love. Even the adrenaline-fueled thrill of the game, the intoxicating dance of risk and reward, had faded into a bitter aftertaste.

He hailed a taxi, the driver a weathered man whose eyes carried the weight of countless sunrises and sunsets. The journey to Miriam's apartment felt like a blur, a silent meditation on the choices that had led him to this point. He knew he couldn't undo the past, but he hoped—desperately—that he could at least offer her some measure of peace.

Her apartment was easy to find, a small but charming place overlooking the sea. He hesitated at the door, his hand hovering over the bell, the weight of his actions pressing down on him like a physical burden. The memories—the echoes of her screams, the silent pleas for mercy swallowed by the night—replayed in his mind with ruthless clarity.

With a steadying breath, he rang the bell. The sound, sharp and insistent, seemed to cut through the tranquil atmosphere, shattering the fragile peace he'd hoped to find. He waited, each second stretching into eternity, his heart pounding a frantic rhythm against his ribs. The door opened to reveal Miriam, her face pale but composed. Her eyes, however, spoke volumes—a mixture of fear, apprehension, and something else. Something that resembled... pity?

The air hung heavy between them, thick with unspoken accusations and unanswered questions. He opened his mouth to speak, but the words caught in his throat. What could he say? How could he possibly explain the inexcusable, the unforgivable? He'd anticipated anger, rage, a torrent of accusations. But Miriam's silence, her controlled composure, was far more unsettling.

"Come in," she said, her voice barely above a whisper, strangely detached. Her expression remained impassive, a mask concealing the turmoil within. He stepped inside, his gaze sweeping over the small, meticulously organized apartment—a stark contrast to the chaotic mess of his own existence.

They sat in silence for what felt like hours, the only sound the gentle lapping of waves against the shore. Finally, Miriam spoke, her voice calm, almost conversational. "Tommy's gone back to New York," she said, her words deliberate, each syllable carefully chosen.

"I... I know," Cohen rasped, his voice hoarse, barely audible.

"He asked about you," she continued, her gaze fixed on the swirling patterns in her teacup. "He wanted to know if you were alright." The irony of it stung. Tommy, the relentless detective, the man who had pursued him with a singular determination, had shown him a kindness he hadn't deserved.

"I'm not alright, Miriam," he admitted, his voice cracking. "I'll never be alright." He watched her, searching her face for some sign of judgment, some flicker of the anger he'd expected, but her face remained unchanged—an enigma wrapped in silence.

Miriam sighed, a long, drawn-out exhalation that seemed to release years of pent-up emotion. "I... I've forgiven you, Sharon," she said softly, her words barely audible. The sentence hung in the air, heavy with unspoken pain and a desperate desire for closure.

Cohen stared at her, stunned. Forgiveness? He hadn't expected it, hadn't dared to hope for it. He had anticipated retribution, justice, but not forgiveness. He didn't deserve it—not even in his wildest dreams.

"But it doesn't change anything," she continued, her voice gaining strength. "It doesn't erase what happened. It doesn't undo the pain. But it's a start. For me."

He nodded, unable to speak. He knew she was right. Forgiveness didn't erase the past. It didn't magically heal the wounds. But it offered a path forward, a sliver of hope in the bleak landscape of his shattered life.

They spoke for hours, spilling out their emotions, confronting the ghosts of their shared past. Cohen spoke of his disillusionment with Mossad, the corrupting influence of power, the descent into a life of crime that had led to his brutal actions. He explained, not to justify, but to clarify, offering a small measure of understanding.

Miriam listened patiently, her eyes reflecting a mixture of sadness and understanding. She spoke of her own struggles—the fear, the betrayal, the long, arduous journey toward healing. She spoke of Tommy, of his unwavering support and his unwavering faith in her.

As the night deepened, the conversation shifted from recriminations to reflection. They talked about the future, about the possibility of rebuilding, of finding some measure of peace. The shadows that had haunted them for so long began to recede, replaced by a fragile, tentative hope. The sands of time, once a symbol of their despair, now seemed to hold the promise of a new beginning.

When Cohen prepared to leave, an uneasy sense settled over him. The forgiveness he had received felt undeserved, a burden almost as heavy as his guilt. He knew the game wasn't truly over. The shadows of his past, the enemies he'd made, remained. His escape from prison, the relative peace he'd found, felt like a mere intermission in a long, brutal play.

The unfinished game continued to play out in the quiet corners of his mind, a constant reminder of the choices he had made and the consequences he would still have to face. The unfinished game, he knew, would find him again. The sands of time were still shifting, still capable of burying him once more. But for now, in the quiet intimacy of Miriam's apartment, a fragile peace had settled—a glimmer of hope in the desolate landscape of his soul. He would keep his eyes open, alert to the slightest whisper of danger. The unfinished game had simply paused, awaiting its next act.

A Final Twist

The relentless Malaga sun beat down on Cohen, its heat oddly comforting compared to the bone-deep chill he'd endured in prison. He'd expected to feel liberated, lighter, but instead, the weight of unspoken truths pressed down on him, suffocating him with their intensity. The email from Miriam had been a lifeline, a fragile thread of connection to the faintest hope of redemption. But no matter how hard he tried, the brutal reality of his past clung to him like a shadow, an ever-present reminder of the man he had become.

He gazed out at the azure expanse of the Mediterranean. Its placid surface, so calm and serene, stood in stark contrast to the turbulent sea of his conscience, a reflection of the inner chaos he could never escape.

Weeks passed in Miriam's apartment, which had become a sanctuary of sorts. She never pressed him for details, never demanded answers. Her silence, however, was more powerful than any confession could have been. It was a silent acceptance that spoke volumes, a deep understanding between them that transcended words. They spent their days together in quiet intimacy, a fragile peace built on the unspoken forgiveness that hung between them. He helped her with her work, offering insights into the darker corners of intelligence gathering—a twisted expertise, born of years of betrayal and violence. And in turn, she reminded him of the man he had once been, the man she had loved, the man he had buried beneath layers of guilt and brutality.

But that peace, however fleeting, was brittle. It was a thin veneer over a festering wound. The hum of Malaga couldn't drown out the echoes of his past—the faces of his victims, the screams of betrayal. They haunted him in the stillness of the night, relentless in their pursuit. He may have escaped prison, but he hadn't escaped himself. He was a ghost, forever tethered to the shadows he had created.

One evening, as the sun dipped below the horizon, casting the sky in fiery hues of orange and purple, Miriam handed him a file. It was thick, unmarked, its contents a mystery. She'd found it while clearing out her desk at the agency—a forgotten relic from an old operation, one that implicated him in ways he never could have anticipated.

The file detailed Operation Nightingale, a Mossad operation he had been tangentially involved in long before his descent into darkness. The official narrative of the operation was clean, sanitized, devoid of the messy, murky realities of espionage. But the file contained a hidden annex, a separate document tucked away, almost an afterthought. In it was a conversation between high-ranking Mossad officials and a shadowy figure known only as "The Architect." The Architect was the true mastermind behind the Al-Qaeda bombing plot—a plot that had set Cohen on his destructive path.

The conversation unveiled a web of deception far more complex than Cohen had ever imagined. The Architect, it seemed, wasn't affiliated with Al-Qaeda at all. He was a player in a much larger game, manipulating both sides of the conflict for his own enigmatic purposes. He had used the Al-Qaeda plot to force the Israeli government's hand, to trigger the removal of their gold reserves from the World Trade Center—a move that, in the end, saved those reserves from the impending disaster. Cohen's role in the operation, his brutal efficiency, had been a critical part of the Architect's plan, but it had all been orchestrated by forces far beyond Cohen's understanding.

The revelation struck Cohen like a physical blow. His life, his choices, the years of violence and betrayal, had all been part of a grander scheme that he had never even known existed. He had been nothing more than a pawn in a game far bigger than himself, manipulated by powers he couldn't even begin to comprehend. The "justice" he had sought, the redemption he had hoped for, seemed to crumble into dust before his eyes.

He spent countless sleepless nights sifting through the information, his mind reeling from its devastating implications. The Architect had remained a shadow, an elusive ghost in the machine, orchestrating events from the darkness. The Mossad, it seemed, knew far more than they had ever revealed. They had knowingly sacrificed him, manipulating his actions to further their own covert objectives. His betrayal of Miriam, his descent into crime—all of it had been expertly staged to divert attention from the true mastermind behind the larger plot, burying his involvement beneath layers of Cohen's escalating criminal activity.

The deeper he delved into the file, the more he realized the scale of the conspiracy. It was a masterfully constructed narrative, designed not only to protect those in power but to discard and sacrifice the expendable pawns. He was not alone in this. The file hinted at other agents, other operatives, who had been manipulated and discarded. Their stories, like his, had been buried, their sacrifices deemed necessary for the so-called greater good.

A chilling thought settled over him like a cold shroud. Had Miriam been aware of this darker truth? Had her forgiveness been part of a calculated strategy, a way to uphold the façade?

He recoiled at the thought. Such cynicism, such cold calculation, seemed too much even for the ruthless world in which he operated.

Days blurred into weeks. He continued his quiet existence in Malaga, but the silence was a lie. The sands of time were shifting beneath him, and the game was far from over. The Architect remained elusive, a phantom lurking just beyond reach, his true motives still a tantalizing mystery. Cohen knew, with an icy certainty, that the game had only entered a new phase—one far more complex, far more dangerous than before.

No longer a player, he had become a pawn—an unwilling ghost caught in a game far greater than himself. The weight of this knowledge was almost unbearable, heavier than the guilt and violence that had haunted him for years.

He reached for the phone, his fingers trembling slightly. He dialed a number he thought he'd never call again—a contact within the Israeli underworld, a man who owed him a debt and understood the language of shadows. He needed answers. Information. Something to help him untangle the web of deceit. He had to understand the full scope of the conspiracy, to know who else was involved.

And perhaps, just perhaps, to find a way to expose the Architect—not for redemption, but for survival. The game had changed, and Cohen had no choice but to adapt—to survive, and maybe, just maybe, to uncover the truth buried beneath the sands of time. The next act was about to begin.

The call connected, followed by a crackle of static and a low, gravelly voice. "Cohen? I thought you were finished."

"Not yet," Cohen replied, his voice barely a whisper, but carrying the cold steel of a man who had stared death in the face and laughed. The game, it seemed, had just begun. The sands of time, he knew, were about to shift dramatically. And he, the pawn in a larger game, was ready to play.

The unfinished game was far from over. It had only shifted its stage, revealing deeper layers of conspiracy that reached far beyond the confines of the Middle East, to the very heart of global power.

The crushing weight of his past, of his guilt and regret, suddenly seemed lighter. No longer haunted by personal demons, Cohen was driven by a new purpose—to expose the Architect, to unravel the conspiracy, and perhaps, in doing so, to find a measure of peace that transcended even forgiveness. The fight wasn't over. It was just beginning.

And this time, he was fighting for more than himself. He was fighting for the truth—buried beneath layers of deception, a truth that could shake the very foundations of the world. The sands of time, he knew, were about to reveal their secrets.

The Mossad, Israel's elite intelligence agency, is known for its stealth and covert operations carried out across the globe. Renowned for its dedication to safeguarding the Israeli people, the Mossad's reach extends far beyond the borders of Israel itself. One of the most secretive agencies in the world, it tirelessly works to gather intelligence and thwart potential threats to its homeland.

In contrast, Al-Qaeda, a global militant Islamist organization, is infamous for its extremist ideologies and violent attacks, including the notorious September 11th attacks on the World

Trade Center. Founded in the late 1980s by Osama bin Laden, Al-Qaeda's goal is to establish a pan-Islamic caliphate through violent means. Despite the death of its leader in 2011, the group remains a potent threat to global security, with branches and affiliates around the world.

The Muslim Brotherhood, a transnational Islamist group founded in Egypt in 1928, seeks to establish a caliphate and promote political Islam. Despite facing opposition from governments like those in Egypt and Saudi Arabia, and being designated a terrorist organization by several countries, the Brotherhood remains a powerful force in the Middle East, North Africa, and parts of Europe.

Meanwhile, the NYPD—New York City's municipal police force—is one of the largest in the world, with over 36,000 officers. Its primary responsibility is to maintain law and order across the five boroughs of New York City. With a long and storied history, the NYPD continues to uphold its crucial role in safeguarding the city, despite facing numerous challenges and controversies over the years.

Mossad remains one of the world's most effective and ruthless intelligence agencies, known for its covert operations and ruthless pursuit of national security. The agency excels at recruiting skilled agents, many of whom are former members of the Israeli military, to carry out its mission.

Al-Qaeda, on the other hand, remains a constant global threat. Though weakened by the loss of its leader, it continues to inspire terrorism worldwide, with its goal of establishing a global caliphate through violent means. The Muslim Brotherhood, similarly, persists in its efforts to influence political change and establish Islamic governance, often through violent means, despite significant governmental pushback.

The NYPD's long-standing tradition of safeguarding New York City continues, despite the city's ever-evolving challenges and the force's complex history. Yet, its critical role in maintaining safety and security remains unchanged, as it continues to protect the citizens of one of the world's largest cities.

Acknowledgments

Writing a novel is often a solitary endeavor, but its success is made all the more meaningful with the support and encouragement of others. First and foremost, I extend my deepest gratitude to my editor, whose insightful guidance and unwavering belief in this project have been truly invaluable. Their patience, expertise, and dedication have shaped this manuscript into something far greater than I could have ever achieved on my own.

Appendix

This appendix provides supplementary information that complements the fictional events depicted in the novel. While the core narrative is a work of fiction, the geopolitical landscape and elements of the criminal underworld are grounded in extensive research. The inclusion of this material is intended to deepen the reader's understanding of the complex realities reflected in the story.

For readers seeking a more comprehensive understanding, further research on the following topics is recommended:

- The history of Mossad operations and their involvement in international conflicts.
- The structure and operations of organized crime syndicates in Morocco and their global connections.
- The history and activities of Al-Qaeda and other terrorist organizations in the Middle East.
- The inner workings of law enforcement agencies, such as the NYPD, in investigating international crime.

Glossary

The Mossad, Israel's intelligence agency, is renowned for its covert operations that span across the globe. This elite agency is dedicated to safeguarding the Israeli people, with its reach extending far beyond the country's borders. Often regarded as one of the most secretive intelligence agencies in the world, Mossad continuously gathers intelligence and works relentlessly to prevent potential threats to Israel's national security.

Al-Qaeda, a global militant Islamist organization, stands as one of the most infamous terrorist groups worldwide. Founded in the late 1980s, Al-Qaeda is notorious for its extremist ideologies and violent attacks, including the 9/11 attacks on the World Trade Center in New York City. Led by Osama bin Laden until his death in 2011, Al-Qaeda continues to be a major threat to global security, with affiliates and branches scattered across the world.

The Muslim Brotherhood, a transnational Islamist organization founded in 1928 in Egypt, seeks to establish a caliphate and promote political Islam. Despite facing significant opposition from government authorities in numerous countries, including Egypt and Saudi Arabia, and being designated as a terrorist organization by several nations, the Muslim Brotherhood remains influential and active, particularly in the Middle East and Europe.

The NYPD, or New York City Police Department, is the largest municipal police force in the United States. With over 36,000 officers and 19,000 civilian employees, the NYPD is tasked with maintaining law and order across New York City. Their responsibilities encompass everything from crime prevention and investigations to offering assistance during emergency situations. The NYPD has a long and storied history, and their unwavering commitment to keeping the city safe has earned them both respect and admiration. Their motto, *Fidelis Ad Mortem*—Faithful Until Death—reflects the deep loyalty and dedication of its officers to one another and to their mission.

References

While this novel is a work of fiction, the following sources provided invaluable background information on the geopolitical context and criminal underworld elements depicted:

Author Biography

Tim Guditus is a former New York City detective with extensive experience in the Middle East and a passion for crime fiction. His background in espionage and intimate knowledge of the region's complex political and social landscape inform the realistic and gritty portrayal of events in this novel. He has spent years researching the intricacies of international espionage and organized crime, translating this meticulous research into compelling narratives. Tim Guditus currently resides in Huntington Station, New York, and is working on his next novel.